Down the Aisle

Down the Aisle

Thomas Varghese

2019

Down the Aisle — published by the Rev. Dr. Ashish Amos of the Indian Society for Promoting Christian Knowledge (ISPCK), Post Box 1585, 1654, Madarsa Road, Kashmere Gate, Delhi-110006.

Online Order: http://ispck.org.in/book.php

Also available on amazon.in

ISBN: 978-93-88945-32-5

Laser typeset by

ISPCK, Post Box 1585, 1654, Madarsa Road, Kashmere Gate, Delhi-110006
• *Tel:* 23866323/22

e-mail: ashish@ispck.org.in • ella@ispck.org.in
website: www.ispck.org.in

Dedication

This book is affectionately dedicated to my beloved wife Lalitha, with whom I have completed 40 years of togetherness in marital life. Her support has sustained me in His ministry. She stood with me through thick and thin and through all challenges in my life and ministry, constantly encouraging me through edifying words of wisdom, valuable prayers and patience – the hallmark of her Godly characters.

Contents

Acknowledgments

Gratitude is the fairest blossom which springs from the soul

Henry W Beecher

It is God's doing in my life one more time that our good Lord has enabled me to revise this book. I am hopeful that it will be helpful to young generation looking forward to get married to have a strong marital relationship irrespective of the difference in many areas in their individual lives. For those who are already married, it may help them evaluate their journey through their marital life and make necessary rectification. I was encouraged to revise this book after observing and counselling many couples who shared their happiness, challenges, and heartbreak experiences.

I am grateful to the Lord Almighty for His steadfast love, mercy and faithfulness for strengthening, enabling and inspiring me to revise this book for the benefit of those who are looking for marriage and for those who are already in this relationship.

I would like to thank Bishop Dr. T. C. Cherian, former Presiding Bishop of the St. Thomas Evangelical Church of India, who wholeheartedly agreed to write the *foreword* for the second edition of the book. He had patiently gone through the entire manuscript in spite of his busy schedule.

I would like to express my gratitude to Dr. Vivian Churness, author of many books, who spend many hours to read, edit and suggest views for the revision of the book in this manner for publication. I still recollect her sincerity and commitment in spending endless hours in editing this book, even while she was at waiting lounges at airports to take connecting flights. We cherish the fellowship and friendship.

A special mention about Mrs. Sheeba and Dr. Sujith Chandy, CMC Vellore, who were instrumental in titling this book.

It is indeed a joy to be associated with the ISPCK team who promptly agreed to publish this revised edition of book, 'Down the Aisle.'

No one has helped me more in revising this book than my wife Lalitha, my faithful partner. We have read, re-read individually and discussed the manuscript collectively for its final shape in this manner. The encouragement of my sons and their spouses who have constantly stood, motivated, prayed so that I could be able to complete this book on time. Also to my four year old grandson Reuben, who enjoyed sitting on my lap and playing with the 'delete' key on my laptop.

My humble prayer is that this book will help many to refresh their marital life and help to prepare others for the holy institution of marriage upholding the vow '*till death do us apart.*'

Foreword

God is not only omnipotent and omnipresent but also omniscient. God's knowledge is unfathomable (Is. 40:28). Therefore all the things God said concerning various subjects and matters recorded in the Bible are infallible, authoritative, true and perfect (Psa. 119:86, 140, 142; Jn. 17:17; Eph. 1:13, 14). What does the Bible teach about marriage and family? Some important facts are given below.

Marriage is not the invention of man, rather it is the first institution of God for mankind (Gen. 2:18f). God established it even before the fall of man. God is the chief celebrant at a wedding service. It is God who unites a man and woman in holy matrimony (Matt. 19:6).

In Malachi 2:14 the word of God says that the better-half of a man is his companion and wife of his covenant. It goes without saying that equally her husband too is her companion and husband of her covenant. Marriage is not a contract rather it is a covenant. This covenant relationship exists till death separates them. The following words of the covenant at the wedding ceremony are worth mentioning. "... until death separates us ... I will be yours and you will be mine and we both will be God's."

Divorce is wrong for three reasons: God hates it. "I hate divorce" (Malachi 2:16). We must abhor what God hates and dislikes. Divorce is breach of marriage covenant. It is against the command of the Lord (Matt. 19:6), "what God has joined together let man not separate." Faithfulness, love, humility, kindness, forgiveness, unity, care, sacrifice, affability and purity are the essential conditions to lead a successful family.

Same sex marriage and homosexuality are ruled out from the divine plan and concept of marriage. God made Eve, a woman for Adam, the first man to be his life partner. (Gen. 2:22). God officiated the wedding of Adam a man and Eve, a woman. (Matt: 19:5, 6). Polygamy and polyandry have no place in the biblical concept of marriage. "The two shall be one flesh". (Gen. 2: 22, 24; Matt. 19:5).

The bridegroom points to the heavenly Bridegroom Jesus Christ and the bride to the redeemed community, the church (Eph. 5:22-23). That means both the bride and the bridegroom must commit their lives to Christ and be imitators of Him.

To lead a family life in accordance with the will and plan of God we need power from above. Holy Spirit is the source of power and prayer is the key to that power. (Lk. 11:13, Matt. 7:7, Psa. 65:2, Psa. 57:2, 1 Thess. 5:18). Prayerless life is a powerless life, prayerless life is an unholy life, Prayerless life is unscriptural life, and prayerless life is a defeated life.

God is the Master Builder of a home (Psa. 127:1). We see God's involvement in the expansion of a home. "Children are a heritage from God, fruit of the womb a reward from Him" (Psa. 127:3). Children are a blessing from God. But with this blessing as in the case of every other blessing a responsibility is attached. Parents must bring up their children in the fear of the Lord (Prov. 22:6; Psa. 119:9) so that they will be a blessing to the family, to the church and to the society at large.

Rev. Dr. Thomas Varghese has studied deeply the subject and presented well the aforesaid principles and additional facts in his book. I congratulate him and wish him all success in the publication and distribution of the book. I am sure that a careful study and observance of the Bible based instructions and suggestions given in this book will enable anybody to lead a sweet and peaceful family life which will be pleasing and beneficial to God and man.

Bishop Dr. T. C. Cherian
25-03-2019

Preface

Marriage, like a submarine,
is only safe if you get all the way inside

Frank Pittman

I am exceedingly glad to write the preface with a deep sense of gratefulness to God the Almighty. All praise and glory to god who grants me wisdom, creativity, time, abundant grace and mercy to complete this project. He leads me!

This book is a revised edition in every means. Obviously there is continuity with previous work, but the structure, content, and some of the thoughts are additional or modified. There are sentences and paragraphs which I have revised to improve the inadequate expression, to give more clarity in thoughts, words and sentences, in growing knowledge and smooth flow of transition. Most of the additions, and improvements have been made by referring books, discussions and based on the comments received from the readers and critics of the first edition. Every principles set forth in the following pages is supported by Biblical precedent. The main thrust of this book is to make people understand and practice the concept of God ordained marriage which is sacred, holy, pure and permanent.

The introductive chapter, I start with a question that many parents are asking, "Is it possible to have a meaningful and stable married life for my son or daughter"? Why do they have these kind of doubts about the stability of the marriage of their children these days? Nowadays, many marriages end up in failure, in most marriages there exist unhealthy relationships due to unresolved arguments, different types of abuse, bitter experiences, separation and finally it ending up in divorce. Can friends, relatives, marriage bureau, marriage counselors, find or choose the right partner for their children?

Choosing a marriage partner depends on individual tastes, inclinations, suggestions from parents or friends. I tried to explain in Chapter 1 about the merits and demerits of arranged marriage, convenience marriage, court marriage, romance based marriage, inter- racial and inter-caste marriage.

In chapter two, a comparative study about marriage ceremonies in various religions in our country is narrated. All major religions teaches one thing in common that marriage is a joining together of two individuals of opposite sexes to a lifelong mutual consent of their sexual qualities as biological, emotional, social, and spiritual achievement and development and which cannot be achieved in separation. All these religions stress on the view of monogamous and permanent lasting relationships.

In chapter three, the focus is on the customs and traditions in the early marriages in our country. The Christians marriage has been viewed as 'a voluntary union for life of one man and one woman to the exclusion of others.' Traditions behind wedding ring, wedding dress, and mangalsutra are explored in detail. The ring is given as a token of love and bonding relationship. It is made in the circular shape which gives the idea of eternity since the ring itself does not have any beginning or ending. The white wedding dress has a twofold implication, according to our forebears as white colour is the symbol of the purity in heart in reverence to God. The 'minnu' (mangalsutra) is initially put on a string made of seven strands of thread taken from the Manthrakodi (wedding saree). The minnu is tied as reef knot around the bride's neck by the groom during the marriage ceremony. This symbolizes the permanence of marriage.

In chapter four, we can see the biblical teachings on marriage, Old Testament teaching regarding the foundational and introductory principle of lifelong union of a man and a woman; which is first recorded in the Book of Genesis. Jesus emphasized in the New Testament the blue print of marriage from Genesis 2:24 as being unconditional, permanent and monogamous. It is God's idea for humanity to be monogamous (Matthew 19:4-5).

The first step in establishing a marriage covenant is leaving all other relationships behind, including the closest ones - father or mother. This is detailed in chapter five, *"Therefore a man leaves his father and his mother."* (Genesis 2:24). The ideology of leaving in marriage is first mentioned in the book of Genesis 2:24. 'Leaving' is not an easy choice and one of the most important choices one may ever have to make in marital life for its abundant blessings.

In chapter six, cleaving, the second essential component of a marriage covenant is explained (Genesis 2:24). Cleaving reflects the central concept of covenant-fidelity. Cleaving confirms the whole hearted commitment from both partners. There should be an unwavering loyalty and faithfulness towards each other which will help them to stay away from marital unfaithfulness, misunderstanding, miscommunications, unnecessary arguments and ill-treatments of all sorts.

In chapter seven, the third essential ingredient of a marriage covenant, becoming 'one flesh' (Genesis 2:24) in other words 'weaving' is detailed.

Chapter eight explores the key to closeness. It knits together the spouses more closely. A good communication will remove all the barriers and the entire vacuum in inter- personal relationships. Good communication does not happen automatically or without any human intervention or by itself.

The next chapter deals with the basic foundations of marriage. Many people are living under the false impression that the marriage will work out automatically without any hard work or preparation. There are plenty of challenges, struggles, painful experiences, and constant repair works. A healthy relationship involves a day-to-day 'commitment' for the rest of the lives with dedication. Marriage is a mutual partnership and team effort by both spouses.

How to resolve conflicts in marriage relationships is dealt with in chapter ten. In most of the marriages, many do not put much effort in sorting and solving issues in marital relationships to mend the relationship. The final outcome will be to discontinue the relationship with the spouse and start a fresh relationship with another person.

Chapter eleven, speaks about marriage counselling. People tend to copy from forefathers, relatives, friends, or neighbors, certain customs, tradition or practices. Many people are unprepared for marriage and confused about the roles, responsibilities, stability and lifelong success in a marital relationship. Hence they need competent help from mature believers, pastors and counselors to give proper guidance for a successful and stable marriage. Pre and post-marital counselling is the need of this hour. Continued support by the church, post-marital counselling, sermons from the pulpit can sustain them in their marriage if they have deep rooted faith. Few sample questions are also included in this chapter.

It is my sincere prayer that this book will be a life changing agent thus *making a difference* in families, church, and society at large in our own country. Let this book be useful in church, women's and youth groups, family counsellors, individuals and families to set strong foundation in the Lord Almighty and foster an abiding relationship with Him.

Rev. Dr. Thomas Varghese (Ivanachen)
July 2019

Introduction

*There is no more lovely, friendly and charming relationship,
communion or company than a good marriage*

Martin Luther, Table Talk

The marriage of Mr. A and Ms. B was the talk of the town for many days. Large flex banners were displayed about the wedding a week before the event. People in the town waited for hours to have a glimpse of the film star and the political leaders who were attending the wedding. To control the crowd extra police were deployed. Another surprise was that the bride and bridegroom arrived in separate white horses and threw garlands on each other from horse back before they entered the church. No words can explain the church decorations; flowers were imported, it was a theme wedding. Dress code and colour specifications were intimated much earlier to the guests and they too obliged accordingly.

The bride was elegantly dressed. The dress was weaved with golden strands and she wore platinum and diamond ornaments. The wedding dress cost many lakhs. One old man said it is only in films he had seen such kind of videography and equipment. Songs were carefully chosen and sung by professional musicians. There was an interruption when one of the State Cabinet Minister entered the church while the message was being delivered. He had many followers and a police force. As usual he was in a hurry to go and so he went to altar, congratulated the bride and bridegroom, greeted the congregation, and shook hands with other dignitaries. Sermon was disrupted for a while till he left the church. The family was extremely happy that this man accepted the invitation and came. For those attending the wedding, it was a time to renew friendships and to meet new people, however they continued doing so inside the church.

After the ceremony, the photography session was a tedious task. The marriage feast could start only after two hours as photo session took a long time. The focus was shifted to entertaining guests, toasting with wine, a sumptuous feast, receiving gifts, and music and dance. The very next day, a photograph and a small write up about the marriage and the dignitaries who attend the wedding was found in all the leading newspapers and on local television. This is a true story that took place in the State of Kerala recently where my family attended.

They are 'DOWN THE AISLE...'

What happened to solemnity and the spiritual aspect of weddings which used to be the focus in the past? Many times I ask the couple what was in their minds when they entered the church and or during the service. Some say they were apprehensive, and had an unknown fear of future. A few admitted that they were quite busy running around making various arrangements and were concerned about the wedding reception. A few others said they could not concentrate but will leisurely watch the video and listen to the sermon. I wonder how much importance they had have given to the service, prayer, message, vows they have taken, sermon, meaningful songs and felicitation.

They are 'DOWN THE AISLE...'

Is it possible to have a meaningful and stable married life for our children in this modern era? This is a valid question raised by many parents. We also hear the cry of many young couples, 'our home has been turned into a war zone' giving us moral insights into the deeper issues families are facing. In earlier days, these questions or comments were not heard loudly. What leads the people to ask this question? Why do people have doubts about the stability of marriage these days more than the past? Probably these doubtful questions arise as they observe many people's lives and experiences in their marriages. A good number of marriages these days are existing with unhealthy relationships, arguments, constant friction, disharmony, abuse, bitterness, separation and divorce be it their neighbors, business partners, church members, rich or poor, educated or uneducated, people of any faith or atheist. In many marriages at the least little problem, the threat of divorce is thought about. Our society has made separation or divorce an easy option to get rid of marital problems rather than finding an amicable solution to lead a peaceful life.

Can friends, relatives, marriage bureau, marriage counselors, event managers, books on marriage or the internet find or choose the right partner? Attractive advertisements are available in the social media about eligible bachelors or attractive women on educational qualification; financial status - bank accounts, house, land and vehicle ownership; spouses family details- traditional families, details about rich and influential family members; opinion or request for live-in-relationships before marriage; detailed explanation on physical structure of the spouse which include skin color, length of the hair, color of eyes, vision, height, weight, various interests in life, hobbies, food likes and dislikes and what they look for in the partner, religious preferences, and future aspirations. Although all information is given in detail, many marriages end up in failure.

Marriage is a socially and Biblically approved institution through which the family is established. Marriage is an essential part of any society. If someone does not get married, his or her not getting married becomes the biggest topic with negative implications questioning why the person isn't getting married. Marriage for some people is a commitment, which they make to the person they love and want to spend the rest of life *till death* with them. However some people get married, not for love; family or a relationship but for other petty reasons. Compared to earlier days there is an enormous change in the views of marriage arrangements, traditions, systems and cultures between the people entering into the marital relationship. People are spending lakhs and cores of rupees on gifts, decorations, food, arrangements and other events.

Marriage is ordained by God where husband and wife give to each other lifelong companionship, help and comfort, both in prosperity and adversity and in sharing joy and sorrow. The church also wants the couples not to have any other relationship, thought, aspiration, or desire that may break their vows and interfere with their family life.

Following are a few definitions of marriage to consider. Dr. S. Radhakrishnan, the former President of India, observed marriage as, "an institution devised for the expression and development of love. Its purpose is not only the generation and nurturing of children but also the enrichment of the personality of the husband and wife through the fulfillment of their need for a permanent comradeship, in which each may supplement the life of the other and both may achieve completeness."[1] Through this definition Dr. S. Radhakrishnan affirms that, "marriage is based on mutual love, commitment, mutual trust and permanent companionship. The spouses enrich each other. There is procreation, and nurturing children is the key factor of marriage relationships.

Through the institution of marriage they achieve completeness in life."[2]

According to Webster's dictionary, marriage "is an institution whereby men and women are joined in a special kind of social and legal dependence for the purpose of founding and maintaining a family."[3]

According to John Stott, "a marriage is an exclusive heterosexual covenant between one man and one woman, ordained and sealed by God, preceded by a public leaving of parents, consummated in sexual union, issuing in a permanent mutually supportive partnership, and normally crowned by the gift of children."[4] In this definition John Stott clarify that marriage is a heterosexual relationship, God ordained one, through leaving, cleaving and weaving, they are saturated to one another. Children is the gift from the outcome of their mutual relationship. The above definitions are discussed in detail in the following chapter.

Marriage can be compared to a fruit garden. The soil in the garden needs ploughing, adequate preparation for seeding, good seed, proper care, enrichment through manure, water and committed farmers. In the same way to receive good harvest in the marriage one needs to sow the seed of uncompromising and unselfish love, peace, patience, kindness, goodness, respect, faithfulness, gentleness, self-control, care, understanding, quality time, and effective communication. A fervent prayer is the basic foundation for a successful and effective marriage. Apostle Paul in Galatians 6:7-8 says, ".....A man reaps what he sows. The one who sows to please his sinful nature, from that nature will reap destruction." In the garden of marriage, there may be good or bad harvest. Seeds in the marriage are planted through the words of communication. Therefore a right word at the right time is highly essential. In order to have a good yielding in the garden, weeding is very important. Therefore we need to weed the hurts, hatred, strife, criticism, anger, selfishness, misunderstanding, ego, and remove the petty issues. Sometimes the plants in the garden of marriage may look fine from outside but not so inside. In order to have a good harvest we need to rectify the mistakes. Rejoicing over the harvest in marriage through leading a peaceful family life, children and the future generation, praising, honoring and glorifying God at the family altar for all his blessings.

Forms of marriage vary from culture to culture. Various forms of marriages are based on the number of wives or husbands a person has. Two broad categories are monogamy (one spouse) and polygamy (more than one spouse).

Monogamy: It is marriage in which there is only one man married to one woman. It is common everywhere. It is the law of our land and the dictate of the church, because it is Biblical and God ordained. It is a dominant form of marriage throughout the world.

Polygamy: It is a form of marriage in which a person may have more than one spouse at a time.

There are two types of polygamy, namely polygyny and polyandry.

Polygyny: It is a form of marriage in which one man marries many women.

Polyandry: It is a form of marriage in which one woman marry more than one man at a time.

Endnotes

[1] Ram Ahuja, *Indian Social System-Marriage in Indian Unit 2* (Jaipur & New Delhi: Rawat Publications, 1993), 27-28.

[2] Thomas Varghese, *Abuse of women in Indian Christian Families-Preventive Role of Church and Theological Institutions* (Delhi: Indian Society for Promoting Christian Knowledge, 2018), 53.

[3] *Webster's Seventh New Collegiate Dictionary* (1971), s.v. "Marriage."

[4] John Stott, *Issues Facing Christians Today - A major appraisal of contemporary social and moral questions* (Bombay: Gospel Literature Services, 1989), 262.

Choosing a Marriage Partner

A happy marriage is the union of two good forgivers

Robert Quillen

"Research demonstrates that people tend to be drawn to others like themselves-people of the same class, race, religion, age, and interest. Of course, there are exceptions, but faced with a wide range of choices, most people choose a mate similar to themselves. This tendency is known as homogamy. Homogamy is the tendency to choose a mate similar to oneself."[1] Choosing a marriage partner depends on individual tastes and inclinations and also on whom one has had occasion to meet.

Arranged marriages

Arranged marriages have played a very important part in the history of the Indian culture. This is the oldest form of planning marriages in our culture and a norm followed in our society. The practice of arranged marriages began as a way of uniting and maintaining upper caste families. Eventually, the system spread to the lower caste where it was used for the same purpose.

One can find a match for arranged marriages through friends, relatives, news- paper advertisements and social media. A marriage is known as arranged where there is active involvement of parents, relatives or friends along with those who are entering into the marriage relationships. They make necessary arrangements for a suitable date for the wedding by the bride and bridegroom's parents or those who are responsible. During the betrothal ceremony it is made sure that the accord between the two families regarding the marriage is finalized. This engagement opens the way for both bride and bridegroom to open up to each other. It also facilitates interaction, clarity and understanding between the two families from the beginning. The marriage service is formal in the case of an arranged marriage and the expenses are mostly shared by both families. Most arranged marriages in the earlier days used to be stable, healthy, happy, peaceful, strong and successful. Marriages and relationships often break down where facts are hidden from the beginning. Arranged marriages have its own merits and demerits. They have a better success rates and less ego related issues.

In this era, many youngsters look at marriages differently. Many of them do not intend to have a lifelong commitment; they do not want any strong tie up with anything. They want more freedom, flexibility, and more space in their marriage with no boundaries. In modern marriages, many partners are not willing to compromise, adjust, evaluate or mend the relationship for a better and long-standing marriage. Social media has a great influence on modern marriages. In the arranged marriage system matching a couple's religion, faith, caste, and creed is merely stacking the odds in favour of marital adjustment although there is no guarantee that marrying the person of the same caste, community and religion is the key to marital bliss. One of the advantages of an arranged marriage is compatibility in family, education, socio-economic level, religion, language and culture. Therefore they can easily communicate without much struggle. Raising children is an easy task. In the arranged marriage the consent of the both parents is there. Therefore, family support is always available, and there is better understanding between both families. In times of difficulty, or unforeseen incidents, the couple can expect help from their parents and in-laws for physical, emotional or financial support. After the arrival of children, in case both spouses are working , finding a reliable babysitter is a non-issue as the grandparents are available to care and nurture the children. If man and woman come from a similar background and share the same views of marriage and family, the chance of divorcing due to irreconcilable differences is not as strong as other marriages. It is very apparent to everyone that the parents' wisdom and consent of the child leads to a happier and healthy union, so divorce would be very unlikely.

There are few disadvantages. Couples may have the inability to make up their own minds freely without interference or dependency on the elders and parents. When difficulties arise it is very tempting to blame one's parents for making an unsuitable alliance. Some marital arguments and conflicts are settled better when only the spouses are involved. When the in-laws or any members of the extended families interfere and impose their views, stress and conflict in the marriage may result.

Convenience marriage

A marriage of convenience is a marriage between two people for legal, practical or financial reasons and not for love, intimacy, companionship or lasting relationship.

This type of marriage involves two people agreeing to marry as a result of a contractual arrangement between the parties. Usually the agreeing party is the woman or her parents. The marriage could be for the person to gain permanent residence in the country where the agreeing party lives or to reduce the risk of being deported back home from that country. In this case, people may not marry for love. They marry a good match for social standing and money. Additionally, if they want to keep the assets in the family, they may arrange a marriage of convenience with a distant cousin. If they were not quite heterosexual, it really didn't matter because they would still pick out a suitable member of the opposite sex to marry.

Often, a marriage of convenience is a mutually beneficial agreement, with both parties profiting from the binding. It may even involve a contract, but not always. Sometimes, only one of the partners may be in it for something other than love.

There are many reasons one may choose to marry for convenience, and can be one or more of the following- when reputation is at stake, to grab the partner's money or to obtain citizenship, marriages are also arranged for a man or woman with psychiatric problems, impotency or infertility, illegitimate pregnancy, any congenital defects, a single parent, out of sympathy, or to please parents. To a great extent these are arranged marriage with or marriage without the consent of the man and woman.

Consanguineous marriage

Consanguine refers to blood relationships. Sanguine meaning 'blood.' Therefore, blood related marriages are called consanguineous marriages. The potential benefits of consanguineous marriage are related more to social factors than to religious or psychological. Two people and their families already know each other well and a high degree of compatibility exists in every aspect. There is less stress and strain on the marriage particularly financial and adjustment issues. One in two rural marriages in Tamil Nadu and Andhra Pradesh are consanguineous. Most commonly, first cousins — uncle's son marries auntie's daughter or vice versa. Scientific studies have shown that consanguinity leads to death of infants before, during or immediately after birth, increased incidence of birth defects, genetic diseases including blinding disorders, blood cancer (acute lymphocytic leukemia), breathing problems for children at birth (apnea), increased susceptibility to disease etc. It is sad to note that many movies in Tamil Nadu and Andhra Pradesh highlight and glorify consanguinity. Evidence suggests that consanguinity does play a negative role in human health. The social benefits of consanguinity should not outweigh the biological damages. Many in the community are ignorant about these facts.[2]

Court marriages

Court marriages in India are fast catching up with the times. These kinds of marriages are becoming popular among educated Indians who do not want to spend money on lavish celebrations. Couples who are forbidden from marrying by family members also go to court to be married. Register marriages do not involve any religious ceremonies and are done in front of the Registrar of marriage and two witnesses. A valid marriage certificate is given to the couple immediately as a proof of their legal marriage. Some of these marriages are held at the convenience of the partners, and some couples start to live together without having any religious function or without the knowledge of family members. Religious ceremonies are not given importance and they insist that marriage ceremonies and festivities are unnecessary extravagances. They hold that all the gratuitous expenses of the marriage can instead be used for a good cause like supporting a poor family for their daughter's wedding or helping to construct a small house for some poor and needy person.

Live-in-relationship

"The live-in-relationship is a living arrangement in which an un-married couple lives together in a long-term relationship that resembles a marriage."[3]

In a 'live- in -relationship' there is no marriage between parties solemnized under any law. They may live together without legal marriage for a few years. This is also known as cohabitation. Cohabitation simply means, living together without any legal binding of the marriage. Yet the parties live as couple and there is stability and continuity in the relationship. It is also known as a 'common law marriage'. They may want to test whether the marriage is workable without any friction or compatibility issues before decisions are made about entering into Holy matrimony. "According to DeMaris cohabitation is also known as trial marriage."[4] The couples agree in advance that there will be no offspring. Medical technology will make it possible for them to live up to that part of the arrangement. Some couples may choose sterilization, and some others will use contraceptive methods.

In urban areas, getting safe accommodations for a single lady used to be very difficult. Having a male partner for security was important once a young woman moved to a city. Having safety and security was one of the early reasons for live-in-arrangements, later leading to live-in-relationships.

There are other reasons for partners to decide to live together : sharing finances equally to reduce financial burden, separation made easy if the need arises, lack of faith in marriage as an institution, peer pressure, for cheap popularity, a marriage not supported by the family due to religion, caste, race, age difference, financial background, educational status, or to preserve their single status in front of family, individuals who are already married and not divorced but desires to live with this person, couple who give priority to career rather than marriage and child rearing, or to escape from loneliness when living away from family. Therefore a live-in-relationship is an alternative for the couple because there is no commitment, no risk, no responsibility, and no time for or with the partner.

"The Allahabad High Court recognised the concept of live in relationship in the case of Payal Katara vs. Superintendent Nari Niketan and others, where in it held that live in relationship is not illegal. The court said that a man and woman can live together as per their wish even without getting married."[5] The Supreme Court of India recognized live in relationship as legal relationship and is not considered as prohibited relationship. The Supreme Court in: Indra Sarma vs. V.K.V. Sarma said, "Live- in- marriage like relationship is neither a crime nor a sin though socially unacceptable in this country."[6] It was an ambiguous concept until the Supreme Court of India took the initiative and declared that a live in- relationship though considered immoral, but not illegal.

Live-in relationships in India have still not received the consent of the majority of people in this country. It is considered as an immoral and an improper relationship. The majority of the Christian community in India neither welcomes the idea nor accept, advise, or permit live- in- relationships as it is contrary to Biblical culture, Godly principles, traditions and customs upheld in this country. It is against the principles of a God ordained marriage. Therefore it is advisable to stay away from this kind of relationship to avoid judgement from the Almighty God.

Inter-religious Marriage

Interreligious marriage is a marriage between individuals of differing religions. In inter-religious marriages there will be differences in religious rituals and tolerance of these differences. Cavan has argued that "inter-religious marriage threatens values, security, and continuity of a religion."[7]

Inter-racial Marriage

Interracial marriage occurs when two people of differing racial groups marry each other. "This is a form of exogamy, marrying outside of one's social group."[8] A simple definition for an inter-racial marriage is the marriage between members of different races. Now a day's interracial marriages are becoming more and more common. All couples contemplating marriage need to give thoughtful consideration to a variety of practical issues, some of which may have no clear Biblical principles or standards.

Faith in Christ, not skin colour, language spoken, is the Biblical standard for choosing a spouse. Interracial marriage is not a matter of right or wrong but of wisdom, discernment, and prayer. Both families may have difficulties in interacting and relating to each other due to differences in language, accent and culture differences. Interracial couples may misinterpret of gesture, tone, language from their spouse and this could lead to serious misunderstanding. Through misunderstanding so many complications can creep into their marriage.

Interracial couples may find difficulty in up bringing their children due to the different background and culture in which they grew up .These differences can bring disagreement between the partners. Interracial couples tend to attract abnormal attention from people. For instance most people stare at them when they are attending a social function in public places. This could make them uncomfortable and they may decide to leave the function before the closing time.

Family members will find it very difficult to accept one's choice of a life partner for their fear of losing their identity and life style, original upbringing, family belief, culture and traditions. Interracial couples tend to experience discrimination from family and friends, therefore there is less chance of acceptance from them.

"Studies do indicate that the trend is changing, and that more and more interracial marriages are occurring between partners who are nearly equal educationally, economically, and culturally."[9] These three important key factors are promoting interracial marriages.

Inter-caste Marriage

Intercaste marriage in India was once considered a taboo and is confronted with unique challenges and protest from the family. However, with the change of time, inter- caste marriages are becoming common among the youngsters of Indian society. Many times we hear that the couples meet with fierce protests and, in some cases, death threats from their own family members. Though the Indian Government has tried to come up with many approaches to change this, not many parents or families are able to understand it and still consider it as an offence.

Inter-cultural Marriage

Inter-cultural marriage refers to the marriage between individuals of two different cultural backgrounds.

Mixed marriages are advantageous to children in many ways. There is a common view that the differences in genetics of children who were born from an inter-caste marriage are smarter than children from a same-caste marriage.

Inter-caste couples are free and more adjustable. They can easily change from the traditional way of thinking because they are in love. They are willing to learn and adapt to each other's culture and values in their daily lives. They are more understanding about various cultural values and differences within their society.

Inter-caste marriages show that people can live in unity and be free despite of various castes and creeds in our society.

The disadvantages of inter-cultural marriages are disapproval by family and society, difficulty of raising children in the mixed culture, children having an identity crisis, and less or no support from the family.

In mixed marriages Christians must be sure to select a partner from the Christian faith, and a Godly person so the couple may live an exemplary family life through a God ordained marriage. Marriage is an institutionalized social and Biblical structure which provides for a healthy sexual behavior within the frame work of a marriage relationship and bearing children.

Second Marriages

Second marriages are different from first marriages. Second marriages take place when there is failure in the first marital relationship or death of the spouse. Sometimes extra- marital relationship end up in divorce, leading to second marriage. The success of second marriages mainly depends on what values and lessons were learned from the break-up of the first marriage.

Romance Based Marriage

Obsession or passion between a man and a woman is not the basis for a permanent and lasting relationship. The greater danger in a marriage like this is that the sexual relationship is often considered prime or more important than anything else. This is an unholy affair, which will surely reduce the very sanctity, and holiness of a true marriage relationship the Bible talks about. This kind of activity will only fulfill one individual's enjoyment, gratification and satisfaction. This relationship is often instantaneous, shallow, fearful, momentary, short-lived and it denies the true purpose of God's ordained marriage. In India, love marriages are increasingly becoming more popular. Formerly, an arranged marriage was the only option for the boy and the girl, but circumstances have changed, with love marriages in vogue among couples. Parents, today have a broader perceptive, and understand that it is mutual understanding and love that matters the most and not economic standards or ethnicity. Love marriages were mostly confined to urban culture but are now part of rural culture. The concept of love-cum-arranged marriages came into picture with the rise of modernity in Indian Society. Earlier, family members had the responsibility of choosing a suitable partner for their son or daughter, but now children prefer choosing their life partner on their own, hence the love-cum-arranged marriages concept came into existence. Concisely, it is a form of love marriage mutually agreed and accepted by both the families. Though parents generally do not object to their child's choice, they end up saying that the person preferred by their child is the choice of God himself. Mostly mixed marriages are a romance based. Marriage is not a human invention; it is the divine original plan of God. Therefore, young people must be very cautious not to degrade God through their marriage. We need to educate our new generation to distinguish right from wrong based on biblical truth for the benefit of the upcoming generation and to save families in the coming years.

Registration of marriages

In 2006, the Supreme Court in the Ashwani Kumar case had observed that marriages of all persons who are citizens of India belonging to all religions should be registered compulsorily in their respective states where the marriage is solemnised. Registration of marriages should be made compulsory under law to prevent marriage fraud, bigamy, child marriage and desertion of women by their husbands.

A marriage certificate is an official declaration and legitimate proof that a couple is married. In 2006, the Supreme Court made it mandatory to register all marriages for safeguarding women's rights. Hence, obtaining a marriage certificate after marriage can have various benefits. To obtain marriage certificate, the groom must be over 21 years of age and the bride must be over 18 years of age. Earlier for Christians, a church marriage certificate was valid proof of marriage. Nowadays this is not valid proof.

A marriage certificate is an essential document. When applying for a passport, opening a joint bank account for foreign travel or visa processing it is required. Hence, a marriage certificate is an obligatory evidence in India.

Endnotes

[1] Stephen Rawlings, *"Perspectives on American husbands and wives,"* Current population reports, special studies series, No:77 (December,1978):23.

[2] *Problems with consanguineous marriages*, (Hindu), 29 April 2004. http://www.thehindu.com (accessed on January 10, 2019).

[3] Dr. Swarupa N. Dholam, "Socio-legal dimensions of 'live-In relationship' in India," (December 10, 2015). mja.gov.in/Site/Upload/GR/final%20article%20 in%20both%20lanuage%20 (1). Asia Pacific Law & Policy Review, Volume 3, (April 2017),2. Accessed on October 13, 2018.

[4] De Maris, Alfred & Lislie, Gerald R, *"Cohabitation with the future spouse: Its influence upon marital satisfaction and communication,"* Journal of Marriage and the Family (February, 1984): 46.

[5] www.helplinelaw.com/family-laws/SLRI/status-of-live-in-relationships-in-India.html

Live-in relationship as a new form of Family (Volume 2; Issue 11) Author-Chakshu Thakrl, LL.B, Bharati Vidyapeeth University, Pune. Co-Author - Amit Chouhan, LL.B, Bharati Vidyapeeth University, Pune. July 18, 2018.

[6] Constitution of India – Wisdom Crux https://www.wisdomcrux. lawtimesjournal.in/index.php/category/constitution-of-india/

[7] Cavan, S. R, *"Concepts and Terminology in Inter- religious Marriage,"* Journal for the Scientific Study of Religion 9/4 (April 1970): 311-320.

[8] http://www.britannica.com/topic/exogamy (accessed on January, 20, 2019).

[9] Todd H. Pavela, *"An Exploratory Study of Negro-White Inter marriage in Indiana,"* Marriage and family Living (May 1964): 209-211.

2

Marriage Ceremonies in Different Religions

*A great marriage is not when the 'perfect couple'
comes together. It is when an imperfect couple
learns to enjoy their differences*

Dave Meurer

India is a nation with variety of religion, traditions, customs and practices. Every religion, marriage has different customs and ceremonies, but they are celebrated with lots of splendor and glory. There are a lot of changes in the practices of today's weddings from the olden times. This is true in most of the States in India. I am discussing about religious customs, traditions and practices with regard to marriage in a few religions.

Hindu marriage

"Hindu marriage is a religious sacrament in which a man and woman are bound in permanent relationship for the physical, social and spiritual purpose of sexual pleasure, procreation and observance of Dharma."[1] Therefore the concept of marriage in Hindu religion is considered to be a very stable and solemn ceremony for a long and everlasting relationship. Marriage is an important social institution and its form and functions change according to change in culture.

There are certain rites which must be performed to complete the marriage ritual. The main rites are *homa* (ritual offering in the sacred fire) *panigrahana* (taking the hands of the bride by the bridegroom) and finally *saptapadi* (the bride and the bridegroom making seven steps together). All these rituals are performed by a Brahmin in the presence of the sacred fire and are accompanied by the Vedic mantras.[2] The marriage may be legally questioned if the above rites are not performed in the marriage.

The three principles of Hindu marriage are *dharma*[3] *praja*, (progeny) and *rati* (pleasure). Sex plays a major role in marriage in many religions. But in Hindu religion, sex is given only last principle out of the *dharma, praja and rati*. Hindu intellectuals consider dharma as the first among the three and also consider it as the highest aim of the Hindu marriage.

Firstly, it is the fulfillment of dharma or religious duties. According to K.M. Kapadia, marriage is primarily for the fulfillment of duties; the basic aim of marriage is dharma. Secondly, procreation. In Hindu families children are given a very important place. According to Rig Veda, the husband accepts the palm of wife in order to get a high breed progeny. According to Manu, the chief aim of marriage is procreation. Thirdly, sexual pleasure. The Hindu scriptures have compared sexual pleasure with the relation of divine bliss. This purpose seeks pleasurable human activities- as recreation, art, and leisure. Kama also includes the pleasure of erotic activities and sexuality that exists within the marriage.[4]

The Hindu marriage ceremony, called the *vivaha samskaras*, contains many rituals and symbols that mark the marital rite of passage. One of these rituals, the *Saptapadi* or 'The Rite of the Seven Steps,' acts as the most defining wedding ceremony act. It constitutes the 'essence of a Hindu wedding,' by validating and religiously legalizing the marriage.[5]

The words of the seven *Saptapadi* at each of the seven steps or circles around the fire, the groom recites for the future of marriage. The first step for *the abundance of nourishment in life,* explains the mutual obligation and duty of the couple to nourish and provide for each other. Through marriage, a couple fulfils a religious duty and receives spiritual nourishment. Many religious observances and rites may only be performed by a married couple. Marriage is after all a sacramental union, according to Hindu thought, rather than a social contract, marriage constitutes a religious institution of two human beings distinguished by a third divine presence.[6] Second step is for strength in life. Third step is for prosperity in life.[7] Fourth step for the fulfillment of all earthly desires.[8] The groom recites the above wish for worldly human pleasures. Fifth step is meant for procreation. In particular, it obligates the couple to repay their ancestral debts. The members of the couple must repay the ancestors who gave them life, and they do so through procreation. Sixth step is for the enjoyment of the various seasons of life. Seventh step is for a lifelong friendship. Devotion and fidelity in marriage remain even upon the death of a spouse. This marks a significant transition in Hindu life. It shows a lifelong commitment of fidelity to another person that must uphold religious and communal obligations. It is no surprise that the Hindu marriage ceremony contains rituals and symbols to mark a momentous occasion. Within each of the seven steps or seven circles around the fire, the saptapadi ultimately embodies Hindu values of the couple's married life that lies ahead.

Islamic marriage

Muslim marriage is known also 'Nikah' in Urdu. The wedding rituals of Muslim marriage vary greatly from the Hindu religion, which emphasizes on the union of two souls. There are even varied rituals performed before and after the wedding.

The first wedding ritual is the *Istikhara,* wherein the religious head takes consent from Allah to perform the wedding. After it is done, the groom's mother visits the bride's house with sweets and *Imam-Zamin,* a silver or gold coin wrapped in silk cloth. It is tied with her onto the upper portion of the girl's hand. This is called *Imam-Zamin* ceremony. The next is *Magni,* wherein the groom's family members visit the bride's house with sweets and fruits. This is reciprocated by the bride's family as well. Nowadays, the couple even exchanges rings.

After this the *Manjha* ceremony takes place, in which the bride is dressed in yellow clothes and turmeric paste is applied to her body. Mehendi ceremony is the next ceremony, which is held on the previous day of marriage. During this ceremony, the hands and feet of the bride are adorned with *henna* designs. Subsequently, the *Sanchaq* ritual takes place, wherein the groom's family sends clothes and jewelry for the bride, to be worn at *Nikah* and *Chauthi.*

On the wedding day, the Baraat leaves for the bride's house. At the wedding venue, they are given a hearty welcome and the groom enjoys a glass of sherbet offered by his brother-in-law. Soon after this, the *Nikah* is commenced. There are two religious heads present at the place, representing the two parties. *Mehar,* a compulsory amount of money, is given to the bride by the groom's family. The *Maulavi* asks the bride three times, whether she accepts the concerned person as her husband, with the amount of the *Mehar.*

After her consent, the groom is asked three times, whether he accepts the concerned woman as his wife, with the decided amount of *Mehar.* After his consent, the *Nikahnama* is signed by the bridegroom and bride, and followed by the recital of *Khutba.* Blessings are showered upon the bride and the groom for a prosperous married life. Following a lavish dinner, the couple is seated facing each other, with their heads covered by a *dupatta*. The Holy Quran and a mirror placed between them, through which they are allowed to see each other for the first time. This is known as *Aarsi Mushaf.*

After the wedding rituals are over, the bride bids farewell. This is called the *Rukhsat* ceremony. On reaching the groom's house, his mother holds the holy Quran over the bride's head as she enters the house. Next is the *Valimah* ceremony, where a grand feast is given by the groom's guardians. Subsequently, the *Chauthi* custom is observed, where the couple visits her parental home for the first time after marriage. They are given a lavish feast and gifts by the bride's parents.

Sikh marriage

Sikh marriage is planned and celebrated for a week. It is simple and it primarily sticks to religious practices. It is conducted in a Gurudwara[9] in front of the Guru Granth Sahib.[10] The religious customs and rituals play an important part of their marriage ceremony.

The first ceremony, *tilak* ceremony[11] is known as engagement. It is the first part of the marriage ritual. The bhaiji[12] recites hymns and offers a date to the groom and applies tilak on his forehead. Gifts are exchanged between the bridegroom and bride's families. Second ceremony is the *chura ceremony,*[13] which takes place at the bride's place. The maternal uncle or aunt of the bride presents red and white bangles to her. Silver and gold ornaments are tied to the bangles which are called *kalirein. Maiya* is the custom wherein the bride and the groom are not allowed to leave their house till marriage ceremony takes place. The next ritual is *gana*, a red thread is tied to the right wrist of the groom and on the left wrist of the bride, to protect them from ill forecast. The third ceremony is called the *vatna* ceremony[14] in which *vatna*, a scented powder made of barley flour, turmeric and mustard oil, is applied to the bridegroom and bride followed by a ceremonial bath. Fourthly, *mehendi ceremony* is organized on the eve of the wedding day. Mehndi is applied on the hands and feet of the bride. *Gharoli* is another pre-wedding ritual, wherein the water from Gurudwara is fetched in an earthen pot for the ritual bath of the groom.

The wedding rituals are brief; a flower veil is tied to the groom's forehead by his sisters. A currency garland adorns his neck, followed by *milni ceremony*,[15] in which both the families meet at the bride's place. They attend the Gurudwara kirtan where shabads are sung and ardaas are recited. After this, the bride and the groom circle around the Guru Granth Sahib and seek blessings.

After the wedding ceremony at the Gurudwara, the bride leaves her family, and this is known as the *vidaai* ceremony.[16] The bride's family bids her farewell as she throws back handfuls of rice over her shoulders. Subsequently a reception party or grand feast is organized by the groom's family in order to welcome the new member to the family and to formally introduce her to family and friends.

Jain marriage

Jains celebrate their marriages with enormous enthusiasm, which are performed with simplicity and sanctity. A grand public proclamation is made with the intention that the bride and groom live together blissfully for their entire life. *Lagana Lekhan* is a small puja, held at the bride's house to decide an auspicious date and time for the wedding by the priest. She is then sent to the groom's house. The reading out of this letter by the priest, at the groom's house is known as *Lagna Patrika Vachan*. This takes place after the *Vinayakyantra* puja is done by the groom. The Sagai takes place at the groom's place, wherein a puja is conducted. The bride's brother applies tika on the groom's forehead and presents him with gifts like gold chain, clothes, sweets, token money etc.

The *Lagan Patrika Vachan* usually takes place after the Sagai ceremony. Next is the *Mada Mandap* ritual, which takes place at the bride's as well as groom's residence. All the rituals are performed by a priest. After this, the Barati and Aarti ritual is held. On the arrival of the barat, the bride's brother applies tilak on the groom's forehead and offers him gifts. The groom also applies tilak on his brother-in-law's forehead and gives him a coconut. Married women from the bride's side perform traditional aarti and sing mangalgeet.

Phere is the most important ritual in the Jain wedding. The bride and the groom are seated in the mandap. The father of the bride performs Kanyadaan or Kanyavaran ritual. He places cash and rice in her right hand and presents her to the bridegroom. While chanting mantras, the priest pours holy water on the hands of the couple thrice. This is followed by *Granthi Bandhan*, in which a married woman ties the knot between the bride's sari and groom's shawl.

After this the *mangal pheras* take place around the sacred fire. During the *pheras mahaveerashtak* strot is recited in the background while the ladies sing *mangal geet*. The couple also takes the seven vows after the *pheras*. After this, the bride is regarded as *Vamangi*, as she becomes the better- half of her husband. Next is the exchange of garlands between the couple.

After the wedding rituals are over, the elders come forward to bless the newlyweds. This is known as *Ashirvada* ceremony. On the arrival of the couple to the groom's house, the bride is given a warm welcome by groom's family. This ritual is called *Sva Graha Aagamana*. As an expression of gratitude, alms are given in the Jain temple. This is known as *Jina Grahe Dhan Arpana* tradition. Subsequently, a reception party is hosted by the groom's family, in order to formally introduce the bride to family and friends.

Jewish marriage

Jewish marriages are performed in a traditional manner. Marriage is a reminder for both partners that they are responsible for each other as well as their religion and culture. It symbolizes more than the mere exchanging of rings. The Jewish wedding ceremony is known as *kiddushin*,[17] which is derived from the word *kadosh*, meaning holiness. A Jewish marriage is preferably conducted on a Tuesday.

Pre-marital rituals include, *Yom* Kippur[18] *Viddui*, the bride and the groom offer prayers to forgive each other for their past individual mistakes before they start a fresh life together. Secondly, *Kabbalat Panim*,[19] wherein the couple is not permitted to meet each other one week before wedding. Thirdly, Badeken[20] tradition, where the bride and the groom see each other as the groom veils the bride, this takes place just before the marriage ceremony.

The wedding ceremony takes place under the *chuppah*,[21] which is an open shelter where the bride circles the groom seven times, which known as *kiddushin*. After the blessings from the betrothal, the couple drinks wine from the cup, followed by the exchange of the rings between the bridegroom and bride. The next is the reading of *Ketubah*,[22] a wedding contract written beforehand and signed by two witnesses. Finally, *Sheva* Berakhot[23] ceremony, wherein the *Rabbi* narrates seven blessings over a cup of wine. A wine glass is placed under the bridegroom's foot and he is asked to break it.

Seudat Mitzwah,[24] is the wedding reception. The Jewish wedding feast contains mouthwatering delicacies. This is followed by Mitzwah dance, wherein all who attend the reception, dances around the bridegroom and the bride. This is not only as an expression of joy and happiness, but also an expression of support from the community towards the bridegroom and bride as they enter into marital life.

Basic Concepts of Marriage
The Hindu marriage ceremony is a religious sacrament for a long-lasting relationship between a man and a woman. It is not virtually for physical pleasure alone, but mainly for the spiritual advancement of both partners. It is sacred; therefore it is irrevocable at any time. The parties involved in the marriage cannot dissolve it by own selfish behavior, attitude or lifestyle. Both husband and wife are bound to each other *till death* happen to one of them. If the wife is alive, she must show her loyalty and faithfulness to husband even after his death. Personal gratification and pleasure are subordinate factors in the Hindu marriage.

Islam religion teaches that marriage is an institution ordained for the protection of the society and in order that human beings may guard themselves from foulness and unchastity. Marriage is a civil contract, the objectives of which are the promotion of normal family life and the validation of children.

Sikh, marriage is considered to be a physical, social, spiritual and legal relationship. It is a sacred union between two souls centred on the Guru. Marriage is a spiritual journey where the husband and wife are trying to help one another in their union with God. It is a sacred bond of mutual help in attaining the heights of worldly life and above also spiritual bliss. It is considered as unity of mind and soul. Marriage institution is the most oldest and natural institution in Sikh religion. Marriage and extended family has been the basis of their social structure.

Jain marriages are performed at an auspicious time. The couple then circles around the holy fire to take the seven vows. " They are to provide home with a nourishing and pure diet, to develop physical, mental and spiritual powers, to increase wealth by righteous means, to acquire knowledge, happiness and harmony by mutual love and affection, to be blessed by strong, noble and virtuous children, to be masters of self-restraint and longevity, to work for the welfare of the family as well as the community, to become true companions and retain a lifelong friendship with each other."[25]

In **Judaism,** the main thrust of marriage is love and companionship and not for childrearing alone. The Jewish view of marriage has two halves *becoming* one, thus completing each other. The process of marriage occurs in two unique phases, namely *kiddushin* (betrothal) and *nisuin* (full-fledged marriage). *Kiddushin* occurs when the woman accepts the money, contract or sexual relations offered by the potential husband. Once the process of *kiddushin* is complete, the woman is legally the wife of the man. This relationship can be dissolved through death of one of the partners or decision for divorce. The mutual obligations created by the marital relationship do not take effect until the process of *nisuin* is complete. Through the completion of the process of marriage through *nisuin*, the husband brings the wife into his home and they begin their marital life as husband and wife together.

All the above major religions teach one common thing - that marriage is a joining together of two individuals of opposite sexes for a lifelong relationship. All these religions stress the view on *monogamy*. "Marriage is the voluntary union for life of one man and one woman, to the exclusion of all others In other words marriage is an act of taking girl as wife by her husband from the house of her father-mother. Marriage is the central, cardinal institution of natural society."[26]

Endnotes

[1] R.N. Sharma, *Introductory Sociology* (Meerut, U.P: Raj bans Prakashan Mandir, 1975), 286.

[2] K.M. Kapadia, *Marriage and Family in India' Hindu Marriage A Sacrament-*(London: Oxford University Press, 1968), 168.

[3] Dharma means achara or the regulation of day to day life. Achara is the supreme dharma and is the basis of Tapas or austerity. It leads to wealth, beauty, longevity and continuity of lineage. Evil conduct and immorality will lead to ill-fame, sorrow, disease and premature death. Dharma has its root. The controller of dharma is God.

[4] Raj Bali Pandey, *Hindu Samskaras: Socio-Religious Study of the Hindu Sacraments. 'Hindu Wedding'* (Delhi: Motilal Banarsidas, 1969), 219.

[5] Ibid., 226.

[6] "Hindu Wedding: The Sacred Rites of Matrimony" *Hinduism Today* 34.2 (April–June 2012): 37-51. ProQuest. Web. 18 April 2014.

[7] Ibid.

[8] Gerald James Larson, "Hinduism in India and America" Ed. Jacob Neusner. *World Religions in America: An Introduction.* (Louisville: Westminster John Knox Press, 2003), 133.

[9] Gurdwārā; meaning 'door to the Guru' is the place of worship for Sikhs.

[10] https://en.wikipedia.org/wiki/Guru_Granth_Sahib It is the central religious scripture of Sikhism, regarded by Sikhs as the final, sovereign and eternal living Guru following the lineage of the 10 human Gurus of the religion.

[11] www.indianholiday.com/wedding-tourism-india/tilak-ceremony.html. Tilak Ceremony is one of the most important Pre-wedding Ceremonies; it holds an important position as regards its auspicious nature in traditional Hindu customs. The Tilak Ceremony varies from one state to another. It is also very different in case of diverse castes and creeds.

[12] The preacher of the Gurudwara.

[13] www.indianbridalhome.com/traditional-wedding-chura-ceremony-in-punjabi-Culture. Traditional Chura wedding ceremony held one night before marriage, maternal uncles will place wedding bangles (chura) to the bride.

[14] indiatribune.com /Sikh-wedding-rituals. Vatna is a ritual celebrated a few days before the wedding ceremony. According to the tradition followed by the Sikhs, vatna, a scented powder consisting of barley flour, turmeric and mustard oil, is smeared to the bride and the groom. This is followed by an auspicious

bath. Mehndi is another pre-wedding ritual organized on the eve of the marriage. During the ceremony, henna (mehndi) is applied on the hands and the feet of the bride.

[15] www.linandjirsa.com/milni-ceremony-indian-wedding-tradition. The Hindi word 'Milan' is derived from a Sanskrit expression meaning "a coming together," giving the Milni Ceremony its definition as a unification of the two families. This tradition occurs in both Hindu and Sikh weddings before the start of the marriage rituals. After the Groom makes his way through the Baraat procession, the Bride's closest relatives welcome him by sprinkling rose water and offering Shagun, a token of good luck.

[16] indiavivid.com/ vidaai-weepy-Indian-ritual/Vidaai, the ritual of tears. It is possibly one of the most sentimental moments in any wedding across the world. The point is bidding Goodbye to loved ones is always difficult. And when it comes to the parents and the bride bidding goodbye to each other that too forever, it becomes a lot more difficult isn't it? In India, there is a dedicated ritual as Vidaai when the bride leaves her maternal home.

[17] Wikipedia Kiddushin, sanctification or dedication, also called erusin (betrothal), the first of the two stages of the Jewish wedding process. Kiddushin, the last tractate of the third order of the Mishnah Nashim.

[18] https://toriavey.com/what-is-yom-kippur Yom Kippur (The Day of Atonement) is the day of repentance, the most holy day on the Jewish calendar. It is a day of fasting, prayer, and reflection. It is the culmination of a period of time during the month of Elul in which Jews are required to take stock of their lives, to ask forgiveness from friends and family, and to take steps toward self-improvement for the year to come.

[19] Kabalat Panim literally means "receiving of the faces." In English it means "reception, which refers to the reception before the actual chupa (wedding ceremony), when the bride and groom and families receive the guests.

[20] Kitzur Shulchan Aruch, 147:3-Just prior to the actual wedding ceremony, which takes place under the chuppah, the bridegroom, accompanied by his parents, the Rabbi, and other dignitaries, and amidst joyous singing of his friends, covers the bride's face with a veil. At this point, it is traditional for the Rabbi to pronounce a blessing upon the couple. The bride wears this veil until the conclusion of the chuppah ceremony.

[21] A chuppah is still considered a basic requirement for a Jewish wedding.

[22] A ketubah (Hebrew: "written thing"; pl. ketubot) is a special type of Jewish prenuptial agreement. It is considered an integral part of a traditional Jewish

marriage, and outlines the rights and responsibilities of the groom, in relation to the bride. Ketubah-Wikipediahttps://en.wikipedia.org/wiki/Ketubah

[23] Literally means seven blessings.

[24] A seudat mitzvah (Hebrew: hwcm tdw[s, "commanded meal"), in Judaism, is an obligatory festive meal, usually referring to the celebratory meal following the fulfillment of a mitzvah (commandment).

[25] The Pheras are the most important of the Jain wedding rituals and they have to be performed at a predetermined time that is considered most auspicious. The couple circles the sacred fire four times where the bride walks ahead of the groom for the first phera and the groom ahead of the bride for the remaining three. While the Pheras are going on, the priest chants the Mahaveerashtak Strot and guests participate in singing the Mangal Geets.

[26] https://www.culturalindia.net/weddings/regional-weddings/jain-wedding.html Accessed on 25/1/2019.

3

Customs, Rituals, Traditions and Regulations in Christian Marriage

The couple who prays together stays together
Unknown

Pre-wedding ritual

Betrothal (Wedding Settlement / Engagement)

In the yester years the engagement was the most important pre-wedding event in Christian weddings. It started with prayers, offered by the clergy or senior member of the church. After making the formal announcement from the groom's side, information about date, time, and place of conducting the marriage was given. A short sermon used to be delivered by the clergy which was followed by closing prayers and benediction. It used to be a small function held at home with relatives, close friends and a few church members. The bride did not attend the function. Dowry, the amount of gold for the bride, demands of other household items and how expenses were to be shared were discussed and finalized. Meals were provided for all.

But now the situation is changing. Nowadays betrothal is almost like a wedding. A large number of people are invited from all walks of life and it has become a very expensive affair- expenses for hiring the hall, decorations, entertainment, expensive dress and ornaments, transportation, food etc. The two families are able to mingle with each other. There will not be any talk on dowry as it is banned by the Court of Law. The engagement is generally followed by a courtship period before the actual wedding date. The engagement is also announced in the local newspapers and television channels if they are rich and affluent people. Recently many are waiving off the betrothal function to reduce the expense.

Banns[1] Publication

The purpose of banns is to enable anyone to raise any canonical or civil legal impediment to the marriage, so as to prevent marriages that are invalid which would normally include a pre-existing marriage that has been neither dissolved, nor declared null and void. It is the public declaration of a proposed marriage, announced in the parishes of both the betrothed. Ideally, it should be announced two or three consecutive Sundays during worship service as most of the people attend the service and the matter is known to the majority of the members. In most of the Episcopal churches the clergy publishes the banns.

Banns are a traditional way of finding out whether there are any objections to the marriage from anyone. Objections, if any, should be given in writing seven days before the marriage to the respective priest of the parish.

Marriage License

The marriage license is usually granted by bishop or head of the church. There could be a number of reasons for a couple to obtain a license. Couples may not have enough leave to wait to complete the church's stipulations, banns not published according to the regulations or they might wish to marry in a church away from their home parish.

Family Get-together

The day before the wedding, church members, relatives and friends gather together for a time of fellowship. The clergy will conduct the prayer meeting.

The prayer meeting includes singing songs, intercessory prayers, and message.

The dinner will be served. This is held in both places.

At the groom's family, the senior family members get the thread ready for fixing the Thali / minnu. Seven threads are taken from the manthrakodi, threads are twined together and the minnu is suspended in it. It is kept safely along with the manthrakodi, ring, offertory and the Bible. At the bride's home, the senior members check the wedding gown, ornaments to be worn, ring, dress for reception, offertory and the Bible. These rituals are practiced by the Syrian Christian families.

Before Going for Wedding Ceremony

Before the bride and bridegroom proceed to church for wedding ceremony there is prayer at their respective homes offered by clergy. Immediate family members, a few church members, friends and relatives attend the same. The clergy bless them following which the grandparents, senior members of the family, Sunday school teachers and teachers who taught them in secular schools or college bless them. The bride and bridegroom then give them a small gift (dakshina) according to their tradition.

Holy Matrimony

The Holy Matrimony is the term used by Christians to define marriage. Christian matrimony is a holy sacrament, officiated by a priest, of uniting a man and a woman and they become one until death.

Almost all episcopal churches have an order of worship for the marriage. Without compromising the biblical doctrine, it is printed by the family with the names of bride and bridegroom, songs of their preference and distributed to all those who are attending the wedding. The order of worship include liturgy, songs, prayers, sermon, and rituals like exchanging the rings, taking pledge, tying the mangalsutra, presenting the wedding garment (manthrakodi), and signing the register.

Groom Entering First in Church

Bridegroom enters the church first and waits for his bride. Christian marriage is to be a reflection of the relationship of Christ to the church, his bride. "Husbands, love your wives, just as Christ loved the church and gave himself up for her" (Ephesians 5:25). This love is to be sacrificial in nature and Christian marriage is depicted as a picture of the union of believers, bride to Jesus Christ, the bridegroom. It shows the analogy between the relationships of Christ to the church. It is emphasised here about the earthly relationship between the husband and wife in marriage. It reveals that earthly marriages are a portrait of the coming church's union with Christ (Ephesian 5:23-32).

When a person comes to faith in Jesus Christ, he or she is united with Christ, and becomes a part of his bride-to-be, the church. Marriage is one of the ways that God physically and tangibly depicts the relationship of the believer to the Lord Jesus Christ. All this is a mystery until the coming of our Lord and the proclamation of the union of believers with Christ by faith. It is the bride groom (Jesus Christ) who chose us to be a part of the bride (John 15:16). It is the bride groom who laid down his life to purchase the bride (Ephesians 5:25). It is the bride groom who is working to perfect and purify the bride, so that he may present her to himself (Ephesians 5:26).

In this relationship mutual submission, a forgiving spirit and a sacrificial way of love all are interlinked physically in our earthly marriage and spiritually with our marriage with Christ in the future. Therefore the bridegroom enters the church first as an initiator to receive his bride.

Bridal Dress

In most of Christian marriages the bride wears a white dress. The white colour is linked with light, goodness, innocence, purity, and perfection. The white wedding dress is a symbol of the bride's purity in heart in her entire life, and in reverence to God. It's also a picture of the righteousness of Christ (Revelation 19:7-8) with regard to the wedding of the lamb. Here is the imagery of a wedding relationship between God and his people, 'the bride.' Christ clothes his bride, the church, in his own righteousness as a garment of fine linen, bright and clean. Bright linen denotes the righteous acts of the Saints.

Wedding Rings and the Pledge

During the 1st century, it was common for the rich and wealthy to wear rings to show their status and position in society. This was for showing prosperity and good fortune in marriage. The gold ring represented financial status, however in this era the gold wedding ring has been replaced by diamond and platinum. Weddings are sacred rituals that have existed since ancient times, joining two individuals into one unified pair. Wedding rings have existed for over one thousand years, symbolizing fidelity, unity, and love. When the couple exchanges wedding rings, it symbolizes the covenant relationship.

The use of rings in wedding ceremonies is traced back to the early part of the fourth century.[2] However, the first explicit description of the ring's usage seems to come from Isidore of Seville, who became archbishop in AD 595. He writes "The ring is given by the espouser to the espoused either for a sign of mutual fidelity or still more to join their hearts by this pledge; and therefore the ring is placed on the fourth finger because a certain vein, it is said, flows thence to the heart."[3]

A ring has the shape of a full circle. It symbolize the eternal quality of love, no one can separate. It is a seal of authority, which demonstrates their submission to God's authority in their marriage *till death*. The circular design is said to represent infinity. The design, material, and shape should be perfect, as you are intended to wear it 'till death do you part'. Although wedding rings don't have a direct connection to religion in olden days, many religious phrases are used in modern weddings.

The design of rings has changed over the course of its existence. When God chose a rainbow, which forms like a circle, as a sign of his covenant with Noah (Genesis 9: 12-16), God said, "This is the sign of the covenant I am making between me and you and every living creature with you, a covenant for all generations to come: and I have set my rainbow in the clouds, and it will be the sign of the covenant between me and the earth" (vv12, 13). This seal of covenant is a visible and reminder of the commitment.

It states in the Church of England 1662 Book of Common Prayer.[4] "With this ring I thee wed, with my body I thee worship, and with all my worldly goods I thee endow: In the Name of the Father, and of the Son, and of the Holy Ghost. Amen". In Jewish tradition, the groom of an orthodox Jewish wedding will traditionally say, "You are consecrated to me with this ring according to the law of Moses and Israel". Other common religious phrases involving wedding bands in modern day include Catholic weddings, with the common phrase "Take this ring as a sign of my love and fidelity, In the name of the Father, and of the Son, and of the Holy Spirit".

The Exchanging of the Rings

The exchanging of rings is the sacred moment in marriage. The officiate will bless the rings before handing them over to the bride and groom. As they place them on each other's fingers, the couple shall say, "This ring I give you in token and pledge of our constant faith and abiding love," or, "With this ring I thee wed," or, "With this ring I wed you, and pledge my faithful love." The ring exchange is only a recent introduction in the Protestant church. In the past only the bride received a ring.

This devotion of marriage as remarked in the Bible is one of the most rewarding earthly pleasures humans have. God urges you to love one another above all else, as he has loved you. The vows the couple say while rings are being exchanged will be a unique reflection of their future relationship.

"I give you this ring as a reminder, that I will love, honour, and cherish you, in all times, in all places, and in all ways, forever." The meaning of most vows is that rings serves as a reminder and symbol of the promise of the relationship. It traditionally ends with the length of the promise, which is usually forever. The vows are customizable and personal. It is important to reflect on what the ring means to you and to communicate that with the vow.

Wearing a wedding ring sends a message to the public that you are married, you value your spouse and keep the dignity of the covenant of marriage. In private it reminds them of their togetherness whether they are physically near or apart. When they are holding or touching the ring it reminds of the beautiful commitment they have for each other. It is also a reminder of their inwardly and outwardly love and the things they do for each other, their vows, and a reminder of their wedding day. It shows that they value their spouse's thoughtfulness. Tertullian (about 160-225), though known as a *rigorist* for promoting strict standards of Christian conduct and for condemning the use of jewellery, seems to have approved of the use of the marital ring. Tertullian lamented the adoption by Roman women of seductive ornaments, but he commends the ancient Romans for teaching women "modesty and sobriety" by condemning the wearing of gold "save on the finger, which, with the bridal ring, her husband had sacredly pledged to himself."[5] This passage suggests that Tertullian viewed the marital ring not as an unacceptable adornment, but as an evidence of modesty and a symbol of a sacred vow to one's spouse for a long and lasting relationships till death.

The ring came into use in Christian marriage ceremonies in biblical times by the Hebrews. The ring was worn as token of love and bonding relationship. Wedding rings were important because of interior inscription and recordings of the marriage contract signed in the presence of the Emperor's image.

The custom also arose, sometime in the middle ages, of connecting the wedding band with the Trinity. "The Anglo-Saxons, during the engagement ceremony, placed the ring on the bride's right hand finger, and transferred it to the left hand finger at the wedding ceremony. The ring was placed by the priest, first on the thumb, then on the index and middle finger in order, in the naming the three persons of the Trinity. Finally, it was placed on the fourth finger, showing that the bride was subject first to the Trinity, and next to her husband."[6] The ring in the circle shape confers the idea of eternity. The ring itself does not have any beginning or ending; it is endlessness, the perfect example of oneness and unity. The circle form of the ring is also the form of the sun, moon, earth and universe which is a sign of holiness, perfection and peace inside and outside. The circle has always had an impact from past traditions to the present as a symbol of completeness.

The wedding ring is an outward sign of the couple's inward eternal and undivided bond, illustrating with a never-ending circle and the eternal quality of love. Therefore, when the couple wears a wedding ring, they demonstrate their submission to God's authority through their bond of marriage. The couple recognizes that God brought them together and that he is intricately involved in their covenant relationship.

When the couple exchanges wedding rings, it symbolizes the giving of resources like time, talents, wealth, ability and emotional feelings to the other partner in marriage. The exchanging of the rings is another sign of their covenant relationship. Therefore, the exchange of rings places an important role in the wedding service.

Let us look at what the Bible says about ring. In Genesis 24:22, the servant of Abraham, Eliezer of Damascus, on a mission for his master, gave the maid Rebecca a *nezem* ("a golden nose ring," although another variant has *nezem* as "a jewel for the forehead"). Next biblical reference to a ring is in Genesis 41:42, where an Egyptian Pharaoh in about 1800 BC, gave his signet ring to Joseph.[7] Obviously, this ring was not for the purpose of adornment, but was given to Joseph for dealing a transaction to show an authority. We are not sure whether Joseph actually continued to wear this ring constantly on his hand. Signet ring would be deemed too large to wear ornamentally upon the finger. Most rings today throughout the Islamic world in the Middle East are signet rings (khatim, 'seals').[8]

Quick! Bring the best robe and put it on him. "Put a ring on his finger........." (Luke 15:22). This is an act which shows a sign of position, acceptance and authority among others. Both James

2:2 and Luke 15:22 use the Greek word *daktylos* ('finger') for 'ring.' This would lead us to believe that the ring would be ornamental. However, in Luke 15:22, where the noun *daktylos* is translated 'ring,' it seems that a signet or seal is indicated. This may indicate that this particular ring is not ornamental, but is rather a restoration of the family seal so that the son is empowered to once more conduct business in the father's name by using his seal on the signet ring. Moreover, concerning the 'ring' in Luke 15:22 it is not specifically mentioned that the ring is made of gold or silver. From the Biblical history we learn that the common people in the Roman Empire were not allowed to wear gold rings during Jesus' day.

The wedding ring is a mark, a reminder and an identification which shows that he or she belongs to an important person. In modern days, this argument does not have much value or merit. The spouse, who truly wishes to make known that they are married, will act morally and modestly in the presence of others.

The purpose of the ring according to Clement of Alexandria was not ornamental, but has a practical and protective factor. It is practical because the wife used the signet ring the husband gave her to seal those goods 'worth keeping safe in the house.' If a servant ran away with some household goods, the seal on them would prove the ownership. The signet ring worn by the wife represented the authority her husband had delegated to her to manage all the household affairs.

In the modern day, rings have become an object of desire and attraction. People fall in love with rings in wedding due to a variety of reasons. People start to wear rings as status symbols, dignity; with sentimental feelings; sign of protection, identification, ownership, certain privileges; exhibiting costly and valuable jewels, fashion etc.

Wedding Pledge

The bride and bridegroom pronounce the vows during the marriage service. This is the most solemn moment in the marriage ceremony. They are making an eternal vow before the Almighty in the presence of those who gathered in Church. They promised to each other before the assembly that they will be by each other's side through all phases of life till death separate them. The vow that bride and bridegroom say as they exchange rings is the unique reflection of their relationship to each other. The bride and bridegroom exchange the ring on the ring-finger of the right hand and while holding hands they take the pledge.

"I give you this ring as the sign of accepting you to be my wife / husband. I honour you with my body, mind and soul. All my respect and status and worldly wealth, I share with you. Before this assembly, and in the presence of God that searches all hearts, I promise you that I will, according to the law of God, love, cherish and satisfy you in weal and woe, in prosperity and poverty, in health and sickness, till death do us part. From this day, I will be yours, and you will be mine, and we both will be God's. To this, may God the Father, God the son and God the Holy Spirit help me. Amen "[9]
" I take you to be my wife/ husband to have and to hold from this day forward; For better, for worse; For richer, for poorer; In sickness and in health; To love, cherish, and protect, till death do us part, According to God's holy law; And to this I give you my pledge."[10]

In the above pledges the following phrase is very common to all denominations: 'for better, for worse; for richer, for poorer; in sickness and in health; to love, cherish, and protect, till death do us part.' This simply means that in every situation of their life they are together till death separates them. This is based on biblical principles.

In conclusion the real meaning of most vows is that the exchange of rings serves as a reminder and symbol of the promise of their unbreakable personal relationship to each other. And also the vows are a message of the love and respect that they have for each other that the couple will live together in peace, goodwill and love, with a promise of unconditional love and fidelity.

Tying the Mangalsutra / Thali / Minnu/[11]

The word, m*angalsutra or mangalsutram* developed from sankrit term *Mangal* which means prosperous, blessed and happy. *Sutram,* means cord or thread. On this thread, a gold thali is strung in the centre. It is an ornament that symbolize marriage in Indian tradition.

The word *talikettu or minnukettu* is considered to be the most public function in the marriage ceremony. *Thali / minnu* is the foremost symbol of the covenant of marriage in India.

The mangalsutra is the symbol of an inseparable bond between the husband and the wife. It is a mutual commitment to each other. The thali / minnu represents a spiritual mark of love, respect, obedience, commitment and dignity which is offered to the wife by her husband. Married women are expected to wear the mangalsutra throughout their lifetime. The mangalsutra acts as a protective covering and protects the marriage from all kinds of evil. The women wearing a thali / minnu around her neck is a mark of respect as she belongs to the man whom she married. Marriage is the union of two bodies and two souls. The bride wears it forever to signify the permanent commitment and loyalty in the marriage. It is removed only just before the funeral. After that it is given to the Church's poor fund.

This act is an ancient tradition, symbolizing mutual trust, love and commitment. The bridegroom ties the minnu around the bride's neck.

The seven threads for the minnu are taken from the manthrakodi (the bride's traditional wedding garment.) The customary practice is that after the minnu is being tied, the manthrakodi is placed on the head of the bride by the bridegroom. Traditionally this is a practice among the Syrian Christians in Kerala. The minnu is shaped in the form of an elongated leaf consisting of a cross in the centre.

The position of the bride standing on the right side of the bridegroom, the bridal garment or sari (manthrakodi) and exchange of wedding rings have possible origins from Jewish temple rites and customs described.[12]

The *minnu* is tied around the bride's neck by the groom during the marriage ceremony. A good way to remember how to tie a reef knot is very simple- tying the thread left over right and right over left. This knot is more or less impossible to unknot or untie- in other words it symbolizes the permanence of the marriage. The ceremony of *minnu-tying* is also practiced by the Jews living in Cochin.

Due to the solemnity after the marriage ceremony, or before going to bed, the *minnu* is put on a gold chain to avoid breaking the cord of the *minnu*. The wife is expected to wear this chain till her death. Having the *minnu-mala (minnu* attached to the chain) is a sign of a married woman. This is meant to give women the security to move around freely without harassment from others.

Presenting Wedding Garment (*Manthrakodi*)[13]

The term manthrakodi originates from two key words- m*anthra,* means blessed and *kodi,* means new cloth. This literally means blessed new cloth, is the special name given to the wedding garment which is presented to the bride soon after the groom ties the *minnu.* Presentation of the *manthrakodi* to the bride at the end of the wedding ceremony marks the completion of the ceremony. *Manthrakodi,* or the wedding garment, is the first gift to the bride in public from the bridegroom, which signifies him as her 'provider' in the coming days. While the prayers are being recited, the *manthrakodi* is placed on the head of the bride by the bridegroom .It is another common tradition in South Indian Christian weddings, which symbolizes the groom's everlasting guarantee of being a 'protector' of his bride for the rest of her life. This act symbolizes that the groom covers her with his love, care and warmth. It also signifies all the responsibilities vested on him to meet or provide physical, emotional, social and spiritual needs for the rest of her life. As soon as it is presented to the bride, the bridegroom's sister or one of the immediate family member comes forward and stand along the couple signifying that the bridegroom's family is publically welcoming her.

In olden times, the woman is expected to keep the *manthrakodi* safe and in good condition till her death. She is to be draped in her wedding sari in the coffin, a tradition practiced in certain cultures even today.

Pronouncement as Husband and Wife

Finally, before the closing prayer and benediction the priest who conduct the wedding ceremony will pronounce the bride and bridegroom as husband and wife. St. Thomas Evangelical Church of India's pronouncement of husband and wife is as follows, "Now, our dearly beloved, beware that you are standing before the Lord, before this assembly, who has purchased through his blood, before the life-giving Gospel, before he that knows the secrets of hearts. From this day, God hath joined you together. For everything you do unlawfully, you have to give account before God."[14]

Pronouncement by the Syrian Marthoma Church of Malabar, "...Now our children, remember that you stand before God's holy altar, before the throne of our Lord Jesus Christ and his holy table, before the Cross, before the holy Gospel, before this congregation, and in the presence of God who knows the thoughts of every heart. From this time onwards, we have united you to each other. May God be the judge between you and me. I shall be free from blame for anything you do contrary to the divine law."[15]

This final pronouncement officially declares that the bride and groom are now husband and wife. This moment establishes the exact beginning of their covenant.

Affixing Signatures in the Marriage Register

Once the marriage is solemnized, the couples affix their signature in the marriage register in front of the great assembly of believers thereby endorsing the marriage. The church marriage register contains the details of bride and bridegroom, their signatures, the signature of the priest who solemnized the wedding along with two witnesses.

Marriage Certificate Registration

Under the Indian Christian Marriage Act, 1872, Christian marriages in India are solemnized by a clergy[16] or minister or priest in the church. Today, along with this church marriage certificate one need to register the marriage with the Registrar of marriages. In order to get a marriage registered and legalized, an application should be submitted to the concerned authority with all details.

Wedding Reception

After solemnizing the wedding service, the couple exits the church with much excitement and happiness surrounded by well-wishers, church members, relatives, and friends. The newlywed couple, along with all the invitees for the marriage, moves to a banquet hall to attend the wedding reception. This is also another joyous occasion for all, especially bride and bridegroom. At the wedding feast the guests propose toasts to the couple's well-being. There will be a time to introduce the bride and bridegroom's immediate families and time to take photographs. There may be short speeches from the best man and maid of honour, following which the wedding cake is cut together by the bride and groom who feed each other before it is distributed among the guests. Then the bridegroom offer thanks to all the people present in the hall. Then invitees then greet the couple.

Wedding Feast[17]
A ceremonial meal has been often a part of the blood covenant in the Old Testament. At a wedding reception, guests are invited to share the joy and happiness with the couple in the blessings of the covenant. The reception also illustrates the wedding supper of the lamb described in Revelation 19:7, the 'wedding of the lamb.'[18]

In the modern era many people prefer to attend the wedding reception than attending the marriage service. It is a relaxing time where they meet friends, renew friendships and fellowship, and have fun and excitement over a sumptuous meal.

Many times it goes beyond the spiritual atmosphere since it is controlled by the 'Event Managers.' They plan according to the requests made by the bride, bridegroom and their respective families. Ear- blasting music, dance, and games are also organized by them.

Visiting Bridegroom's House
The immediate relatives of the bride will be visiting the husband's house on the same day after the wedding feast. The mother-in-law welcome the daughter-in-law extending her right hand and daughter-in-law is expected to put her right foot first as she enters her husband's home. Refreshment will be served during this time.

Then bridegroom presents a costly sari /clothes to the mother-in-law and for senior members of the wife's family. The mother-in-law, in return, presents him gold ornaments. Gifts are exchanged by other family members also.

Visiting bride's family

On the third day the bride's parents will visit the groom's family and take the couple home. During this time the couples will be visiting their immediate families and friends. Some of them invite them for meals.

Nowadays the couple plans for honeymoon trips immediately after the wedding reception. They may return after a fortnight or so, make a quick visit to their parents and are off to their working places. They postpone visiting friends and relatives to a later date because of their busy schedule setting up their own home and re-joining work.

Endnotes

[1] http://en.wikipedia.org/wiki/Bans of marriage

[2] Isidore of Seville, "De Ecclesiastics Officiis 2, 20," in *A Dictionary of Christian Antiquities, note 19,* Volume 2, 1807-1808.

[3] Ibid., 1808.

[4] *The Church of South India: The book of Common Worship*, Second Edition (Madras: Oxford University Press, 1979), 141, 142.

[5] Tertullian, *Apology 6* (note 16), Volume 3, See also Tertullian, *On Idolatry 16, The Ante-Nicene* Fathers Volume 3, 71 (Grand Rapids, Michigan: Zondervan Publication,1973), 22.

[6] William H. P. Phyte, *5000 Facts and Fancies,* (New York: G.P. Putnam's sons, Kicker bocker Press,1913), 641.

[7] Henry H. Halley, *Bible Handbook* (Grand Rapids, Michigan: Zondervan Publcation.24th Edition, 1965).

[8] Yedida Kalfon Stillman, *Palestinian Costume and Jewellery,* (Albuquerque: University of New Mexico Press, 1979), 103.

[9] *St. Thomas Evangelical Church of India, Order of service-Holy Matrimony* (Manjadi, Thiruvalla: Silver Jubilee *Press*, 1996), 9.

[10] *The Church of South India: The book of Common Worship*, 141, 142.

[11] The night before the wedding service, seven strands of threads are drawn from the manthrakodi (wedding garment) and twisted to form a cord. Minnu or mangalsutra is tied on this cord, a leaf shaped gold pendant with a cross.

[12] Professor George Menachery, *St. Thomas Christian Encyclopaedia of India* (Trissur, Kerala, 1973).

[13] As per the tradition of Syrian Christian, during the close of the wedding ceremony the bridegroom present a new sari to his bride. This sari is known as manthrakodi. It is placed on the bride's head with this sari.

[14] St. Thomas Evangelical Church of India, *Order of service-Holy Matrimony*, 19.

[15] The Marthoma Syrian Church Of Malabar, Hoothama-The order of Worship Holy Matrimony (Thiruvalla: Marthoma Press, 2013), 64, 65.

[16] Clergy means ordained and licensed by the Church.

[17] The Wedding Feast is arranged in a church hall or nearby hotel or other reception hall. This is for the bride and bridegroom's family, friends, relatives, and well-wishers who are invited for the marriage.

[18] The Wedding of the Lamb mentioned in Revelation 19:7 is the imagery of a wedding to express the intimate relationship between God and his church. Church is considered as 'his bride.'

4

Biblical Teachings on Marriage

*Committing to staying calm is the first key
to committing to staying married*

Hal Runkel

It is believed that God, the creator instituted marriage and conducted and blessed the first wedding in the Garden of Eden. We can boldly say that God the Almighty officiated the first marriage. When we compare it with the new generation marriages, it was less extravagant in terms of expensive wedding arrangements, settlement, wedding dress, ornaments from silver to platinum, dowry, theme based decorations, costly reception hall, presence of distinguished guests, video and photography, feasting with varieties of food items, gifts, expensive transportation system and publicity through social media etc.

If marriage is ordained by God, then one enters into this covenant relationship with him and pledge to always submit to his authority. These key factors are missing in many marriages today. Therefore, marriages end up in failure, misery, separation or divorce. The success of any marriage does not occur automatically but through the hard work of both partners, along with the blessing of Almighty God.

In every God ordained marriage there are at least three important grounds of understanding. "The first and the foremost level is 'unity of spirit' - the oneness of heart and soul in God. In this oneness we can have community not only with our spouse but with all believing persons. The second level is 'unity of emotion' - the current of love from one heart toward another that is so strong that a person can, so to speak, hear the heartbeat of another. The third level is 'physical unity'- the expression of oneness found when two bodies are fused in perfect union."[1]

How two different individuals becoming one flesh? It is a great mystery. Many couples are satisfied with the physical and emotional levels of their marriages. However, a marriage is not based strictly on physical and emotional unity alone. Both partners have a different role to play in the marriage. If couples are happy only with these two components, their marriage will turn to be frustrating and disappointing, even though waves of emotional or physical attraction are normal and natural.

God Ordained Marriage

God ordained marriage is seen in the book of Genesis "For this reason a man will leave his father and mother and be united to his wife, and they will become one flesh" (2:24). This verse very clearly and specifically affirms that God's original intention of marriage is monogamy. The God ordained marriage is a binding relationship with a man and a woman.

Old Testament Teaching

The foundational and preliminary principle of lifelong union of a man and a woman, is first expressed in the Book of Genesis. The Old Testament portrays a number of couples : Adam and Eve (Genesis 2:15-3:13); Abraham and Sarah (17:1-8,15-22,21:1-7); Isaac and

Rebekah (24:26-67); Jacob and Rachel (29:1-30); Boaz and Ruth (Ruth 2:1-13,4:1-17); Elkanah and Hannah (1 Samuel1); David and Abigail (1 Samuel 25:14-42); and Hosea and Gomer (Hosea 1,3).

The Old Testament presents marriage as a divine institution till eternity. God is the designer of marriage. Therefore, God has every right to tell us which principles should govern our marital life and its relationships. Humans were created as sexual beings, consisting of male and female as equals. This means that though men and women are sexually and functionally dissimilar, they enjoy the same dignity, significance, and importance before God. Genesis 2:18 states, "...I will make a helper suitable for him." Literally, "a helper in corresponding by way of supplement to the incompleteness of his lonely being, and in every way adapted to be his co-partner and companion."[2] God designed woman to be man's suitable and proper helper, - a helper supportive to him always - a like-minded and supportive personality. Thus, the basic foundations for the divine institutional marriage is man's physical, spiritual and emotional need, and woman's power to satisfy that need.

The first marriage is recorded in Genesis 2:22, "...the Lord brought her to the man." We can conclude three different consents from the above passage. First, the *father's consent,* which consists of God's ideal provision for the lonely man- Adam. Second, the *woman's consent* - Eve surrendered to God's plan when she was brought to the man. Third, the *man's consent* - Adam joyfully received and welcomed the best gift from God and said, "...bone of my bones and flesh of my flesh... (Genesis 2:23)." These are the central concepts of the first marriage in the Garden of Eden. Without these three elements, human marriages are sinful in nature and not long lasting. According to King Solomon the bonds of the marriage covenant are also known as the covenant of God (Proverbs 2:17).

The noble characters of woman are mentioned in Proverbs 31:11, "Her husband has full confidence in her and lacks nothing of value." "...She is her husband's crown." (Proverbs 12:4). She brings mercy, grace, glory, honour and delight (4:9). Scripture never degrades or disgraces the woman. The woman was not created to be a man's slave, but rather his co-worker and helper. The term *ezer* means helper does not imply that a woman is a mediocre or a second-rate human being. She is identical in character or personality, worth and value, reflecting the same divine image (Genesis 1:27). Yet she is different in function and role, serving as a supportive co-worker or partner.

God commanded man to multiply his descendants and fill the earth (Genesis 1:22; 9:1). Therefore, heterosexual marriage has been God's normative model of society for reproducing descendants. Much of the Bible assumes marriage is an exclusive heterosexual pledge and mutual relationship between one man and one woman.

New Testament Teachings
Jesus emphasized the blue print of marriage based on Genesis 2:24 as being unconditional, permanent and monogamous relationship.

A marriage union not only fills the need for companionship, but it enables a man and a woman to have a fuller, more complete and perfect personality. Therefore, human beings should not alter God's plan. When we violate God's plan then we are offenders in God's sight. The Scriptures condemn same sex marriages. However, homosexual practice, same sex relationships or marriages are sinful activity according to the Bible although it had been legally approved by the Law of the land in many countries. It is condemned in Leviticus 18:22, 20:13; 1 Corinthians 6:9, 10. In Romans 1:24, 26, and 28 thrice it says, "... God gave them over." "God gave them over in the sinful desires of their hearts to sexual impurity........." (v24), "God gave them over to shameful lusts. Even their women

exchanged natural relations for unnatural ones.'(v26)" ".....God
gave them over to a depraved mind, to do what ought not to be
done."(v28). Nevertheless, none are excluded from God's judgement.
The Apostle Paul reiterates in 1 Corinthians 3:9-10, that the offenders
are not allowed to enter to kingdom of God.

The Bible compares marriage between a man and a woman as
similar to the relationship between Christ and his church. Husbands
are to love their wives in the same way that Christ loved the church.
The scripture concerning the husband-wife relationships is seen in
Ephesians 5:22, 25. Stephen Clark points out the significance of
these two admonitions in his book 'Man and Woman in Christ',
"The New Testament presents only two explicit commands for
husbands and wives. It says that the wife should be subordinate to
her husband, and that the husband should care for his wife. It is
helpful to realize how vague the explicit New Testament teachings
are for what husbands and wives must do. It is also enlightening to
see that subordination (with its correlate-care) is the key element that
the New Testament stresses. Any presentation of the New Testament
teaching on husbands and wives which leaves out subordination has
neglected one principle that the New Testament explicitly enjoined."[3]

The Nature of Biblical Marriage

Marriage is a covenant and is known as a formal accord to engage
in or abstain from a specified action. In a covenant marriage, the
following truths are available.

In a covenant relationship one becomes part of the other
individual and there is a mystical joining of two lives as one. 'Two
becoming one flesh' is a profound mystery but it is an illustration
of the way Christ and the church are one (Ephesians 5:32). The
apostle Paul vividly speaks about the union of Christ and his bride,

the church. When God entered into a covenant with Noah, he gave Noah the rainbow, which was to be a testimony that God would remain forever faithful to keep the covenant never again to flood the earth to tear down all flesh. In Genesis 9:16 the Lord God testified that "Whenever the rainbow appears in the clouds, I will see it and remember the everlasting covenant between God and all living creatures of every kind on the earth." In Genesis 17:5, 15 when God reaffirmed his pledge with Abram, God said "No longer will you be called Abram; your name will be Abraham, for I have made you a "father of many nations" (v5). "As for Sarai your wife, you are no longer to call her Sarai; her name will be Sarah" (v15). "I will bless her and will surely give you a son by her. I will bless her so that she will be the 'the mother of nations;....." (v16).

As the wife takes on her husband's name, the change symbolizes the supernatural identity and oneness God anticipated for the partners who had entered into the marriage covenant. Now, many women do not want to add their husband's name to their original name as they fear losing their original identity. Changing surname after marriage is a matter of personal choice, deep rooted values systems, time consuming and expensive. Changing name in all documents is a lengthy procedure due to the governmental norms or other rules and regulations. If a woman has added her husband's surname after marriage, and then decides for divorce, it becomes difficult to get back her maiden name. As precautionary measure few women may decide to retain their original name due to the alarming rate of divorce in our country. In order to honour a person's religious deity after religious conversion, name may be changed. However it is purely the decision of the woman.

Biblical covenants were often observed with a fellowship meal. This is also known as a "...covenant meal." (1 Corinthians 11:24, 25). The most famous 'covenant meal' is found in the New Covenant where we read that the Lord Jesus on the night he was betrayed took bread and when he had given thanks, he broke it, and said, "This is my body, which is for you; do this in remembrance of me." (v24) In the same way, after supper, he took the cup, saying, "This cup is the new covenant in my blood; do this, whenever you drink it, in remembrance of me" (v25).

Purpose of Marriage

The purpose of marriage can be summed up in three P's, namely Purity, Procreation, and Partnership.

Purity

Elizabeth Elliot said, "Purity means freedom from contamination, from anything that would spoil the taste or the pleasure...It means cleanness, clearness—no additives, nothing artificial—in other words, 'all natural' in the sense in which the original designer designed it to be." Purity must involve the whole personality - physical, spiritual, social, and emotional. Another term for purity is holiness. It must be a complete lifestyle of an individual, being blameless in every area of life. It can be achieved by the power of the Holy Spirit and through prayer life.

One must sustain a spotless, transparent life in his marital life, physical and spiritual fulfilment and the prevention of immorality (1 Corinthians 7:1-7). 1 Corinthians 7:2 says, "But since there is so much immorality, each man should have his own wife, and each woman her own husband." Again in 1 Corinthians 6:18, "Flee from sexual immorality. All other sins a man commits are outside his body, but he who sins sexually sins against his own body." Do you not know that your body is a temple of Holy Spirit, who is in you, whom you have received from God? You are not your own; you were bought at a price. Therefore honour God with your body. (1

Corinthians 6:19, 20). In Proverbs 5:18, "May your fountain be blessed, and may you rejoice in the wife of your youth." It simply means that one must enjoy the woman whom you are married to when you are young and have sexual union with her. In Ecclesiastes 9:9a, "Enjoy life with your wife, whom you love, all the days of this meaningless life that God has given you..." In Hebrews 13:4, Paul likewise said, "Marriage should be honored by all, and the marriage bed kept pure,..." God, the creator knows which kind of experiences will best satisfy humans and which will not; for this reason God condemns physical intimacy outside marriage.

The apostle Paul in I Thessalonians 4:3-8 gives a call to sexual transparency. The sexual sin troubles those who are involved in it. God called us, "...to live a holy life" (v7). "He who rejects this instruction does not reject the man but God, who gives you his Holy Spirit" (v8). Therefore, the reason for chastity is that God called us for holiness. Another reason for sexual purity is that God has given the Holy Spirit to believers for their consecration. Therefore, to live in sexual wickedness is to discard God, and his instructions.

In Romans 1:18-32, apostle Paul talks about the shame and impurity in same sex relationship. To live in sexual immorality is to reject God and his plan for better marriage. There are three basic strategies from the Bible one must understand very clearly, before bringing sexual role in a healthy marriage.

The First is Homosexual Behavior (Romans 1:26, 27)

The word 'homosexual' derives from the Greek *homos* and Latin *sexus*. The scripture clearly states that this is against God's intention of sexual behavior in the holy marriage. Homosexual behavior and attitude is sinful in God's plan. There are several Old Testament references to homosexuality: Genesis.18-19, Judges 19:22-26, and Leviticus 18:22; 20:13. Basic references from New Testament are from Romans 1:26-27, 1 Corinthians 6:9-11, and I Tim. 1:9-11. The above passages condemn adultery, rape, prostitution and lust. In Leviticus 18:22 "Do not lie with a man as one lies with a woman; that is detestable." Again, in Leviticus 20:13, it says "If a man lies with a man as one lies with a woman, both of them have done what is detestable. They must be put to death; their blood will be on their heads."

The Second is Premarital Sex

The Greek word *porneia* means, 'illicit sexual intercourse.' Premarital sex means having sexual relationship before marriage. This activity is considered as an immoral sexual behavior and Bible clearly condemn this conduct. When a person indulge in sexual activities before marriage, they may focus on the 'recreation aspect of sex whereas if it is within the marriage, along with recreation aspect, there is another aspect procreation.'

The apostle Paul in 1 Corinthians 6:18 says, "Flee from sexual immorality. All other sins a man commits are outside his body, but he who sins sexually sins against his own body." The very next verse reminds us "...... that your body is a temple of the Holy Spirit" (v19). Immoral behavior is against God's guidelines. Again in 7:8, 9, "......It is good for them to stay unmarried, as I am. But if they cannot control themselves, they should marry, for it is better to marry than to burn with passion."

The Third is Extra-marital Sex (Galatians 5:19)

This relationship will not bring the couples united together but cause them to fall apart. This is sinful because it breaks the vows of holy matrimony between two people, disturbs their bond of marriage, violate the partner's right, and create permanent wounds physically, spiritually and emotionally. If a person or persons commit this act, the only way to get out is through repentance, forgiveness, and reconciliation.

Chastity is a great word we must always remember when we think about God's holiness and sex as described in the Bible. It refers to accepting and to implementing true sexual morality, whether we are young or old, male or female, married or unmarried, priests or laity, in public or private life. Therefore it means to keep sexual activity according to a Godly standard. According to C. S. Lewis, the Christian standard is "either marriage with complete faithfulness to your partner or else total abstinence."[4] According to Daniel R Heimbach, "God honoring sex is pleasing - it pleases God and it pleases us-which is exactly what God intends. He cared so much about making sex pleasing that he wrapped physical pleasure, emotional satisfaction, psychological fulfillment, spiritual meaning into one complex relationship."[5] A good, healthy, and meaningful sexual relationship is seen in the Song of Songs. The apostle Paul also urges the Christians in the Corinthian church to stay away from sexual sin, by saying "...honour God with your body" (1 Corinthians 6:20). He also warns very seriously, "... the sinful desires of their hearts to sexual impurity for the degrading of their bodies with one another" (Romans 1:24).

Sex in marriage is personal and relational. It is designed to express a meaningful, joyful and holistic relationship between both spouses.

Procreation
In Genesis 1:28 we read God telling Adam and Eve, "...Be fruitful and increase in number; fill the earth and subdue it." In Jeremiah 29:6 God said, "Marry and have sons and daughters; find wives for your sons and give your daughters in marriage, so that they too may have sons and daughters. Increase in number there; do not decrease." In 1 Timothy 5:14, Paul said "So I counsel younger widows to marry,

to have children, to manage their homes and to give the enemy no opportunity for slander." From the above verses, it is obvious that God expects procreation through marriage. People who marry but do not have children miss one of the greatest privileges that God has given to humanity. Through procreation, it opens up a new way to provide a moral foundation for the future of humanity.

According to Andreas J Kostenberger, "procreation is considered as an integral part of God's plan for marriage. There are marriages where some couples do not have any children due to various health problems. Some believe that childlessness is a curse from God. It is not true at all. However, this point of view poses some ethical problems because a childless marriage is not perceived as inferior."[6] Procreation "is of secondary importance because a childless marriage can also be a blessing."[7]

Malachi 2:15 states, "...because he was seeking godly offspring. So guard yourself in your spirit, and do not break faith with the wife of your youth." Malachi declares that an important purpose of marriage is to produce godly offspring. Biblical marriage sanctifies the children (1 Corinthians 7:14) and children must be trained in the ways of the Lord Jesus (Matthew 19).

Partnership
The apostle Paul in Ephesians 5:23-25 says the purpose of marriage is for mutual help and guidance. Genesis 2:18 saying, "It is not good for the man to be alone. I will make a helper suitable for him." Therefore, God made a companion for man. It is none other than his own wife, which is God given. Jesus also said, "For this reason a man will leave his father and mother and be united to his wife, and the two will become one flesh" (Matthew 19:5). Becoming one is a process that only occurs in the security of your commitment to your loved one. We need to not only recognize that marriage is to drive out

loneliness and insecurity but it's also vitally important to recognize that the Bible describes marriage as 'A Covenant of Companionship.' This companionship drives out many evil things from the life of the couple. The word 'partner' means the idea of 'one that has a close, intimate relationship to another.' That is what marriage is meant for - a close foster companionship and intimate relationship between a man and a woman. The word 'partner' here carries the idea of 'union, association' (Proverbs 2:17, Ez.16:8). This marriage covenant is affirmed before a cloud of witnesses (Deuteronomy 30:19). This covenant was witnessed by heaven and earth (Psa. 50:1; Isa.1:2). A 'Covenant to Companionship' to become one flesh also requires a commitment to become one another's companion spiritually, emotionally, recreationally, and sexually. The prophet Malachi directly connected this covenant commitment with God's ultimate intention that two people would find companionship. "The Lord has been witness between you and the wife of your youth… she is your companion and your wife by covenant" (Malachi 2:14). The word companion in this verse means one with whom you are knit together. Love in marriage focuses on giving one's spouse the partnership he or she needs to eradicate loneliness.

When we study the Bible on marriage it is considered as a sacred covenant and not as a contract. The meaning of the terms 'covenant' and 'contract' will help readers to understand Christian marriage in comparison to other religions. Here Paul E. Palmer clarified the disparity between the two, "contracts engage the services of people; covenants engage persons. Contracts are made for a stipulated period; covenants are forever. Contracts can be broken, with material loss to the contracting parties; covenants cannot be broken, but if violated, they result in personal loss and broken hearts... Contracts are witnessed by people with the state as guarantor; covenants are witnessed by God with God as guarantor."[8] In a nutshell, a contract may be broken anytime during or after completing the agreement, but a covenant is unbreakable and a permanent pledge by humans in the presence of the Almighty God for a lifelong unbreakable relationship, till death. This will end only when one of the partners, or both die. The covenant relationship is only possible through the three important components of marriage covenant mentioned in Genesis 2:24, 'leaving', 'cleaving' and 'weaving-becoming one.'

The Biblical order of the family

Headship is an Christological and theological term which is rooted in Ephesians 5:23, "For the husband is the head of the wife as Christ is the head of the church, his body, of which he is the Savior." Here is an analogical relationship of Christ to Church, same way the husband to his wife. According to the Greek-English Lexicon by Bauer, Arndt, and Gingrich, *kephale* means, "in the case of living beings, to denote superior rank …. of the husband in relationship to his wife."[9] 1 Corinthians 11:3, "...the head of every man is Christ, and the head of the woman is man, and head of Christ is God." In Ephesians 5:23, it says that "the husband is the head (*kephale*) of his wife." The word 'head' refer to the concept of honour. Therefore Christ honours God, man honours Christ, and woman honours man. Here head means the spiritual headship.

For the purpose of this study it is better to differentiate here the concept of 'leadership' and 'servant leadership.' Leadership, "the process by which an individual or group influences another individual or group for the purpose of achieving a common vision."[10] The concepts of headship known as 'servant leadership' come from the Greek word *kephael*. But servant leadership, "a process of leaders and followers partnering together for the purpose of achieving a common vision in which the good of the led are placed over the good of the leaders."[11] Therefore, husband and wife are mutually working together for a common aim, vision, goal and life style of their own for the glory of God.

A Chinese saying says, "man is the head of the family, woman the neck that turns the head." The flexibility of the neck is very important for the head for free movement. The head and neck are both essential for the body. The head is attached and rest to our human body by the neck. The bones of the head play a vital role of supporting the brain, sensory organs, nerves, and blood vessels and protecting from mechanical damage. The muscles of the head and neck perform many important tasks, including movement of the head and neck, chewing and swallowing, speech, facial expressions, and movement of the eyes. The neck muscles support the head, and allow for head and neck movement. It serves as the shock absorber between the body and head. In other words, neither neck can function alone nor the head without the support of neck and no human can survive without these vital organs. This concept can be compared to the husband and wife relationship for a successful marital life.

Husband needs a wife who is with him not only spiritually, emotionally and socially but also physically for necessary support in joy ,pain or sickness, trusting him, appreciating him, cheering him, believing in his capabilities, complimenting him on as he goes out into the world every day. As a wife, a woman is expected to stand close to her husband as his beloved, trustworthy friend to build teamwork in establishing happy, healthy and god-centred family. As a mother, she is expected to be an educator and supervisor for her children to provide them with spiritual, emotional and physical strength to fight against evil forces and for various types of challenges ahead of them. As a manager, she is expected to make home comfortable and well-managed for all members of the family.

The Hebrew word *Rosh* as 'Head' is used in a more literal sense in Genesis 3 where we read that the seed of the woman will strike the snake's head. *Rosh,* which means 'chief person' and 'leader'. The terms 'Authority and Rule' mentioned in Genesis 1-3 although these words apply equally to men and women as they have the same authority.

Raymond C. Ortlund,[12] states that both male–female equality and male headship, properly defined, were instituted by God at creation and remain permanent, beneficent aspects of human existence. He defines 'male headship' in terms of responsibility and leadership: 'In the partnership of two spiritually equal human beings, man and woman, the man bears the primary responsibility to lead the partnership in a God-glorifying direction.' He writes, ' ... was Eve, Adam's equal? Yes and no. She was his spiritual equal and, unlike the animals, 'suitable for him.' But she was not his equal in that she was his 'helper.' Ortlund seems to think that 'helper' is a synonym for 'assistant' or 'auxiliary.' He goes on to say, 'A man, just by virtue of his manhood, is called to lead for God. A woman, just by virtue of her womanhood, is called to help for God.' His understanding of 'help' and 'helper' does not take into consideration how the Hebrew word *ezer* ('help / helper') is used throughout scripture.

Headship of husbands does not mean that man has the absolute control over woman. According to the apostle Paul in Ephesians 5:28, "...... husbands ought to love their wives as their own bodies." His love for her is more than physical. It must be the same kind of sacrificial love Christ has for the church. And again in 1 Corinthians 7:3, "The husband should fulfil his marital duty to his wife, and likewise the wife to her husband." Therefore he may not deprive her of what she needs for her happiness and well-being. The apostle Peter instruct husbands to be considerate as you live with your wives, and treat them with respect as the weaker partner and as heirs with you of the gracious gift of life, so that nothing will hinder your prayers. Spiritual fellowship can hinder through rejecting God's instruction concerning husband-wife relationships in the family. Under the umbrella of the Biblical headship mutual submission according to Ephesians 5:21, "Submit to one another (Man and woman or husband and wife) out of reverence for Christ." Indwelling of the Holy Spirit makes mutual submission possible. The accountability of the man to his wife is to protect, lead and provide and the responsibility of the woman is to comfort, teach and nurture the children.

Christ has the authority and power over every man. Man must be under the subjection of Christ. Man is always under the Lordship of Christ. Therefore, man cannot run the show as he likes. He is to be accountable to Christ for every action, deed or decision he is making. The husband holds a position of authority, therefore, is to be honored by his wife. The Godhead of the Trinity is equal in deity (divinity and holiness) and dignity (self-respect). God, the Father, God, the Son and God, the Holy Spirit has a role to play though they are one. In the marital relationship, oneness is essential for a smooth relationship between spouses, oneness in spirit rather than divided in spirit.

According to John Stott, "Headship expresses care rather than control, responsibility rather than the rule."[13] Stott clearly states that man's headship over the woman is primarily for care, concern, love, warmth and help her fulfill her responsibility as a loving wife. The husband is responsible or accountable for the welfare and well-being of his wife. Again, in his statement he explicitly says that headship of man is not to control or rule his wife, but to serve as Christ served the church. Male headship means that, "man bears the primary responsibility to lead the partnership (between man and woman) in a God-glorifying direction."[14]

Through headship, God was given the spirit of accountability to entrust to Adam, but he was unsuccessful and failed in that trust due to the enticement of the serpent, which led to sin. The role and the influence of Satan troubled both of them. Headship in marriage is a God-given responsibility to feel affection for one's wife by empathetically leading her, providing for her, defending her, and honoring her as a fellow heir of the grace of life. The biblical headship is not dictatorial. It is a two-way system. The Bible firmly instructs that a husband is the head of his wife. What does this really mean? What kind of leadership is implied here? Why is this leadership only given to husbands? Why is the word 'head' used for the leadership in the family?

"Headship is not the consequence of the fall. It existed in God's original design. Man was created directly from the Godhead while man had a part in creating Eve."[15] Ephesians 5:32, "This is a profound mystery - but I am talking about Christ and the church." The relationship between husband and wife is illustrated through Christ's relationship to the church. Consequently, the husband–wife relationship is not to be ignored and needs to be taken very seriously.

Headship does mean that man is to cherish and nurture his wife as his own body. His love for her is more than physical. It must be the same kind of sacrificial love Christ has for his church. " Husbands, in the same way be considerate as you live with your wives, and treat them with respect as the weaker partner and as heirs with you of the gracious gift of life, so that nothing will hinder your prayers." (1 Peter 3:7). The spiritual fellowship with God, others and his own wife can be hindered through disobeying, rejecting, or discarding God's instruction concerning this relationship.

The apostle Peter in 1 Peter 3:5-6 presented Sarah as an example of a submissive wife. She addressed Abraham as master. The word 'master' is not a superior or inferior term, it is a word of respect through sincere love. In the modern world, people are afraid to use this term due to ego. The character of submissiveness must be reflected inside of an individual than outside pressure. This character of submission is not dictated by any one, it must come from the heart by itself. It is an ongoing process without much struggle. Her life speaks to us, "Your beauty should not come from outward adornment, such as braided hair and the wearing of gold jewelry and fine clothes. Instead, it should be that of your inner self, the unfading beauty of a gentle and quiet spirit, which is of great worth in God's sight." (1 Peter 3:3-4). Christians should not completely rely on the outward adornment of beauty. Sarah succeeds over her husband with her excellent behavior, and not with her physical appearance as spiritual beauty is more impressive role than outward physical beauty. Her life style is to be submissiveness to God. Submissive to God automatically lead to submissive to husband.

A healthy, well-built, strong marriage stands out here in Genesis 17:18-21, which talks about Sarah's blessings. Always remember that whenever one spouse receives a blessing, reputation or honor, it should be a cause for rejoicing, jubilation and happiness for both partners and not one alone. Anytime resentment or feelings of jealousy arise, it reflects a competitive spirit or a rebellion in the marital relationship rather than being a joint venture. Rebellion always causes strife, disharmony, unpleasantness and separation. This is unhealthy and it always breaks down the marital relationships.

In Genesis 21:12, But God said to Abraham, "Do not be so distressed about the boy and your maidservant. Listen to whatever Sarah tells you..." Sarah's orders about Ishmael were used by Paul as binding Scripture in his teaching about law and grace (Galatians 4:30).

The children of God must submit to Christ as Lord. We are not our own but are bought with a price of his precious blood (1 Corinthians 3:23; 6:19-20; Ephesians 5:23-33). He has all authority in heaven and earth (Matthew 28:18). He is the head of all principality and power (Colossians 2:10). People who wander from Christ are like those who have lost their heads (Colossians 2:18-19). Without the proper head no nourishment or growth is possible (Ephesians 4:15; Colossians 2:19). Paul was not dealing with philosophical speculation in his headship analogy.

Therefore what should be the role of husband? He is considered as the leader, master and head of the family. He is the role model for his wife and children with godly characteristics; further the protector and provider and he nourish and cherish them.

Nourish means, "to provide with the food or other substances necessary for growth and health, also to keep a feeling or belief in one's mind for a long time."[16] The duty of the husband is to provide needed things for growth, and uphold a harmony and peace in the home throughout all their days together.

How does Christ nourish the husband? " .... graciously give us all things" (Romans 8:32). He gives everything what is needed on day today basis. He feeds and satisfies completely (John 6:35). "...holy in sight, without blemish and free from accusation" (Colossians 1:22).

Then how can a husband nourish his wife. In order to nourish, one must be in constant communion with Christ, must seek, experience, gain, enjoy, and participate in Christ. Pray for her and with her daily and read God's word together and do devotions regularly at the family alter. Be an example and lead her softly and tenderly. It is not only for the physical and spiritual *provision* for your family, it is also for the physical and spiritual *protection* of your family.

Cherish means, to love and have high regard for someone more than yourself. People can love, can take care, or have concern for each other, without cherishing one another. To cherish is more than all the three put together - love, care and concern. It means to keep them first in one's mind, value them more deeply, to appreciate, and be grateful and thankful for them, to treat them gently or be mild in nature. Cherish can be compared to wax being applied on the floor making it shinny and tidy. In the same way, we are to cherish relationship with your spouse, to make it look inwardly and outwardly beautiful. This love will protect her from all deteriorating factors of marriage.

Cherish is to treat a person with tenderness and affection, to nurture with care, to protect and aid, to make them happy and to make them feel pleasant and comfortable. We must have a pleasant countenance when we contact people. We should be happy and rejoicing. Cherish is to warm or soften; like a bird sitting on a nest providing safety and security.

How does Christ cherish a husband? He provides security and safety (Romans 8:35-39). His acceptance as child of God (Ephesians 1:4). His compassion, forgiveness and mercy (Luke 15, Lamentations 3:22-23, Psalm 23:6).

How can a husband cherish his wife? Take initiative and pursue her passionately, to understand her needs thoroughly, to provide a place of safety and security, providing undivided attention, finding relaxing time together, appreciating her, willing to give up interesting programme in the television / internet, spending time together with friends, active listening, consider her opinion, pay attention through eye contacts, meeting her emotional needs, be with her in crowded places, let her know you admire her talents and personality, show respect take time to be alone with her, be a spiritual leader in your home.

The role of the husband is to protect his wife. **Protection** is "the act of protecting or the condition of being protected."[17] The husband must protect his wife in every way. Physical protection of his wife is highly essential especially today when reports of rape, crime and abuse against woman are an everyday occurrence. Therefore, as a faithful husband, one need to render protection from every evil thing. Spiritual protection means giving spiritual nourishment through the word of God and constant prayer and creating a good spiritual atmosphere at home. To maintain this atmosphere, the husband must commit his life to the master and Saviour Jesus Christ. Not only the physical protection but also spiritual, emotional and mental protection is needed for the wife. If any time she is down with fear, worry and anxiety, as a loving and caring husband he must encourage, uplift, and edify her.

Affection is defined as "a tender feeling toward another; fondness."[18] A husband must show sensitivity towards his wife by never being rude in his behavior or never using any unkind words to her. Encourage her good qualities and talents as much as possible for the benefit of a healthy and happy home. Affection is the greatest pre-requisite in the life of woman. For the woman affection represents safety, calmness, security, protection, comfort, and support. It is an indispensable reinforcement factor in any smooth human relationship. It simply means to take care, defend or guard even in adverse situations of life. When a person is considered important in one's life, it is important to make our affection obvious through words. In the book of Song of Songs 4:1-11, Solomon cautiously and genuinely puts the words in a proper order. Admire and tell her; it may be her physical look, or quality, or behavior, or what she does. The man must ask his wife for help in expressing affection by giving hugs, dinner out, opening the door for her, holding hands, and going for walks together. It is important for men to have interest in different physical contacts in a non-sexual way. For the husband, it may not be easy to think and demonstrate affection without sex, but at the same time for women, it is difficult to partake fully in sex without an atmosphere of affection.

Maintenance "means of support or livelihood."[19] He must look after her physical, spiritual, and emotional wellbeing by providing and supporting her livelihood. However, some husbands are very lazy and never go to work. They simply sit idle and the wife has to run around to make money. In the olden days the husband was the bread winner. Now women have become active participants in providing for the family. The husband's role is not one of a controlling authority, but more of an overall supervision of the home; not for self-glorification but for the glory of God.

We need to carefully look at what the Bible says about women, how she should be as a wife in order to have a God-centred family life. Jesus always had concern and regard for the woman. Never in his ministry was he against women.

In Ephesians 5:21, 22, 24; cf v 31, **Submission** (*Hupotassomai*) means "obedient, humble, yielding graciously to the power and authority."[20] The character of Christ is an example of inclusive obedience through absolute submission; Satan's nature is just the opposite and one of rebellious behavior. Rebellious nature is simply revolting against the authority and God's plan. This is the common strategy of Satan. The apostle Paul in the epistle of Ephesians Chapter 5 gives us three most important Biblical principles for the submission of wife to her husband. Firstly, submit to one another out of 'reverence for Christ' (v21), wives submit to your husband's 'as to the Lord' (v22), 'as the church submit's to Christ' so also wives should submit to their husbands in everything (v24). The subject matter of verses 21 to 25 emphasizes that honoring God means to put God first in your life. Apostle Paul is adding up the idea of egalitarianism by telling the followers of Jesus Christ to give priority for others. (See Colossians 3:19; 1 Pet. 3:7; Galatians 3:28, 29).

An accommodative wife must acquire the qualities of self-respect, but she must respect and act in response to her husband's compassionate leadership. A caring wife will encourage leadership by showing her admiration. When her husband makes a suggestion, she can decide to accept it graciously or if she does not approve the idea, speak her point of view with respect.

A proper understanding of the word *hupotassomai* (be subject) is essential to a reasonable exegesis of the marital relationship explained in Ephesians 5:21-33. On the one hand, some argue that the content of *hupotassomai* for the wife is equivalent to the love commanded for the husband[21] and indeed, there is a relation between the ideas. On the other hand, others take *hupotassomai* as the equivalent to 'obey' and we surely must explore these similarities and distinctions. Just what does *hupotassomai* imply for the wife? In verse 21, Paul says, 'Submit to one another out of reverence for Christ.' Reverence means to show respect, admiration, appreciation, or high regards. This verse talks about the mutual submission or submission to each other under the influence of the Holy Spirit and not by the influence of any ego. This mutual submission is only possible when we respect, appreciate or show high regards for each other irrespective of the other person's weakness or inability. We need to accept others as they are. This is only possible through agape love and not any other means of love or methods. In verse 18, we are instructed to "... be filled with the Spirit," v19...spiritual songs, v20 ...making music in your heart to the Lord v20 ... giving thanks to God. When possessed with all the above characters, it is not very hard to submit to one another (v21). Therefore, one's submission is under the control of the Holy Spirit and not by one's wisdom or muscle power. In verse

22, wives, submit to your husband as to the Lord.' As a result, the wives of any culture or faith must submit to their husbands as an act of submission to our master and Saviour Jesus Christ.

Then the question comes, 'How can I submit to a dishonest or drunkard or immoral husband?' The answer to the above question is v22 and it is seen in 1 Peter 3:1-7, 'Submission when the husband is an unbeliever.' Submission does not indicate a woman must have the identical view or be in harmony with everything her husband says or does. The Bible does not say that. However, in 1 Peter 3:1, it specifies that she is a believer and he is not. Thus, this means that she disagrees with him on the most important principle of all. Her understanding of final authenticity (authority) may well be utterly different from his. This indicates that submission is perfectly compatible with self-regulating thinking. The woman in this passage has heard the gospel, assessed the claims of Christ, and embraced his atoning work as her only hope. Her husband has likewise heard the gospel and 'disobeyed' it. She thought for herself and she acted. And Peter did not tell her to move away from that commitment. Submission does not mean giving up all efforts to change her husband. A transformation must be according to the Biblical standard for God's glory, and not to the woman's standard. Changing her husband is not the target. This passage is enlightening for a wife on how she might 'win' her husband to the Lord according to godly principles. Peter envisions submission as the most effective tool or approach in changing the husband. Submission to a skeptical husband does not mean a wife gets her personal, spiritual strength from him. The Bible does not say that. When a husband's spiritual development and guidance is lacking, a wife is not left powerless. She must seek the face of God constantly. She is to be nurtured and strengthened by her hope in God (v5). Submission to an unbelieving husband is not to be done in fear but in the freedom in Christ (v6b.) Nevertheless, she must trust in God (Proverbs 3:25-27). God will shield the godly from all harm.

In English word usage, 'submission' means, 'the act of lowering.' *Mittere* means 'to send under' and from Latin, mission 'to lower.' Therefore it is an act of submitting to the authority or control of another. The word *subordination* means "to place in a lower order or class or controlled by the authority."[22] Therefore subordination is to be placed in or occupying a lower class, rank, or position. It is helpful to reflect on a variety of instances of submission in the New Testament in the middle or passive voice. We perceive submission to husbands (Colossians 3:18; Titus 2:5; 1 Peter 3:1, 5; 1 Corinthians 14:34;[23] elliptical: Ephesians 5:22, 24b), to parents (Luke 2:51), to civil authorities (Romans 13:1, 5; Titus 3:1; 1 Peter 2:13). The apostle Paul says in the last part of v1, '… it is established by God.' Consequently, we need to respect them in every way, even though they are different in nature and behavior (1 Corinthians 16:16; 1 Peter 5:5). This theme of submission runs throughout 1 Peter 2:13-3:6. Peter may have the foot-washing scene of Jesus (John 13) in his mind while he is talking about submission here, slaves to masters (Titus 2:9; 1 Peter 2:13, 18). In 1 Peter 2:13, 'Submit yourselves for the Lord's sake to every authority…' The apostle Peter urges that Christians submit to all legitimate authorities whether or not those individuals are believers or not. This verse clearly says that submission is a clear character of every Christian and must demonstrate that in their day to day life through every walk of life. Submission is part of every healthy human relationship. Without the spirit of humility or submission, there is no long lasting amicable relationship. A team spirit is essential in the marital relationship or at home. The spouses must continually be in the process of building each other up from day one, and not tear down the relationship.

One of the good qualities of team building leadership is that it is not about creating a super hero model. It always eliminates super hierarchy. Team building process cannot function if one decides to control another. Through the spirit of oneness and humility, it can be possible. Submission means to have one located over the other, either with a natural authority (parents, slave masters, civil authorities) or a supernatural authority (disciples over demons, or Christ or God overall). In Ephesians 5:21 and 1 Corinthians 14:32, Paul talks about submission to a fellow Christian temporarily, while he or she is exercising a charismatic gift or ministry to the community, in recognition that he or she is speaking for God (cf. 'in the fear of Christ,' Ephesians 5:21), and is in this function 'placed over' the others.

In Genesis 22:1, 'God said to him, 'Abraham!' and he replied, 'Here I am.' Abraham's tone was that of a servant to a master. This same tone of obedience is an example of a voluntary submission before a higher authority, applicable even in our marital relationships. It is also interesting that *hupotassomai* can connote the idea of 'respect.' In Hebrews 12:9 we read, "We have had earthly fathers to discipline us and we respected (*enetrepometha*, imperfect middle indicative) them. Shall we not be much more subject (*hupotagēsometha*, future middle indicative) to the Father of spirits and live?" Here 'to respect'[24] is used in parallel with 'to submit oneself.'

For every meaningful and everlasting relationship, submission plays a key role, which stands for submitting to earthly parents, heavenly master, civil authority, church authority, and husband and wife relationship. The lack of healthy submission leads to argument, blame, finding fault in each other, confusion, and unresolved marital problems. In every sincere submission there should be an element of respect, love, concern, sacrifice, and obedience.

Biblical reasons for a wife to submit to her husband regardless of education, status, custom, culture and practices are narrated below.

First and foremost, man was created first. 'For it was Adam who was first created, *and* then Eve' (1 Timothy 2:13).

Secondly, it is the source of creation. God formed man and all creation in this world directly out of dust, whereas woman was created out of the man's rib. Then the Lord God formed the man from the dust of the ground, and breathed into his nostrils the breath of life, and the man became a living being" (Genesis 2:7). Woman is the only living thing not made from dust. Woman derives her origin from man. "The Lord God made a woman from the rib he had taken out of the man, and he brought her to the man" (Genesis 2:22). "For man did not come from woman, but woman from man" (1 Corinthians 11:8).

Thirdly, it is an underlying principle of creation. Woman was created for man "Neither was man created for woman, but woman for man." (1 Corinthians 11:9).[25] God expects her to be the co-worker and accompanying person (Genesis 2:20-24). Thus she is to honor her husband by submitting to him as the head (v3).

Fourthly, man named woman. Adam named the animals and was to rule over them. "...out of the ground all the beasts of the field and all the birds of the air. He brought them to the man to see what he would name them; and whatever the man called each living creature, that was its name" (Genesis 2:19). "....Rule over the fish of the sea and the birds of the air and over every creature that moves on the ground" (Genesis 1:28). When Eve was brought to Adam, he named her and said, "This is now bone of my bones, and flesh of my flesh; she shall be called woman, for she was taken out of man" (Genesis 2:23).

Fifthly, the principle of entrustment. God directly commanded Adam, " You are free to eat from any tree in the garden; but you must not eat from the tree of the knowledge of good and evil, for when you eat of it you will surely die"(Genesis 2:17).

Sixthly, woman was inclined to sin first. The apostle Paul in 1 Timothy 2:14, "And Adam was not the one deceived; it was the woman who was deceived and became a sinner." Now the serpent was craftier than any of the wild animals the Lord God had made. He said to the woman, "Did God really say, 'You must not eat from any tree in the garden'?" Genesis 3:1. Both passages show the influence of the Satan. He is creating a doubt in the mind of Eve regarding God's warning.

Seventhly, God reproaches Adam first after they ate the prohibited fruit. Although Eve was the logical person for God to rebuke first, God went to Adam, showing that God considered Adam the 'head of the family.' "But the Lord God called to the man, 'Where are you?" Genesis 3:9.

Lastly, woman is the glory of man. "….he is the image and glory of God; but the woman is the glory of man"(1 Corinthians 11:7). The next chapter explains the three important components of a marriage covenant God placed before us through his establishment of marriage as mentioned in Genesis 2:24, "…a man will leave his father and mother and be united[26] to his wife," and they will become one flesh.

Endnotes

[1] Johann Christopher Arnold, *Sex, God And Marriage* (Farmington, Pennysylvania: Plough Publishing House, 1996), 21, 22. *http:www.plough.com* and *www.ploughbooks.co.uk*

[2] Very Rev. Canon H.D.M. Spence & Rev. Joseph S. Exell, eds, *"Genesis"* The pulpit Commentary. (New York & Toronto: Funk & Wagnalls Co.), 50.

[3] Stephen Clark, *Man and Woman in Christ* (Ann Arbor: Servant, 1980), 94-95.

[4] C.S. Lewis, *Mere Christianity* (New York: Simon & Schuster, 1980), 90.

[5] Daniel R. Heimbach, *True Sexual Morality-Recovering Biblical standards for a culture in Crisis* (Secunderabad : Authentic, 2004), 137.

[6] Kostenberger, A J God, *Marriage and Family: Rebuilding the Biblical Foundation* (Wheaton, Illinois: Crossway. 2004), 98.

[7] Douma (1993:123) argues this point thoroughly against the background of the views of Augustine and Barth regard procreation as the primary purpose of marriage. The problem with this view which was held for a long time in Christian ethics is that it reduces marriage to a mere physical relation and implies that the childless marriage is inferior.

[8] Paul E. Palmer, "Christian Marriage: Contract or Covenant? "*Theological Studies* vol. 33, no. 4 (December 1972), 639.

[9] Bauer, Arndt, and Gingrich, *A Greek-English Lexicon of the New Testament and Other Early Christian Literature*, Fourth Revised and Augmented Edition, (Chicago: The University of Chicago Press, 1952), 431.

[10] Justin A. Irving, Definition to key words, "Servant Leadership" Servant Leadership and the Effectiveness of Teams. March 2005.

[11] Justin A. Irving, *Definition to key words*, 2005.

[12] Raymond C. Outland "Male-Female Equality and Male Headship, Genesis 1-3", *Recovering Biblical Manhood and Womanhood: A Response to Evangelical Feminism,* John Piper and Wayne Grudem (eds) (Wheaton, IL: Crossway, 1991), 86–104.

[13] John Stott, *The Message of 1 Timothy and Titus* (Downers Grove, Illinois: Inter Varsity Press, 1996), 225-226.

[14] Raymond C. Outland, "Male-Female Equality and Male Headship," .95.

[15] Mouser, William E. Mouser, *Five Aspects of Man* (Waxahachie, TX: International Council for Gender Studies, 1992), 4, 5.

[16] *Concise Oxford English Dictionary* (2008), s.v. "Nourish."

[17] *Collins English Dictionary – Complete and Unabridged* (2000), s.v. "protection."

[18] The American Heritage® *Dictionary of the English Language*, (2000), s.v. "affection."

[19] *The American Heritage® Dictionary of the English Language* (2009), s.v. "maintenance."

[20] *DK Oxford Dictionary, Revised & Updated illustrated* (2008), s.v. "submissive."

[21] David Fennema, *Reformed Rev* 25(1971) 62-71. He prefers to substitute the word "devotion" for subjection" 65.

[22] *Webster's Seventh New Collegiate* Dictionary (1972), s.v. "subordination."

[23] Submission to husbands is probably the reference here, cf. verse 35; Cf. *hupotagē* in 1 Tim 2.11. Here the reference is also probably the husband (*Andros*, verse 12, though it is anarthrous).

[24] *Entrepō*, with the middle sense, "turn [oneself] towards something or someone, have regard for, respect" (Arndt and Gingrich, p.269, 2b). It is used with *phobeō* in Luke 18.2, 4: "neither feared God nor regarded man." It is used of respect for superiors or men of power in the NT (Matthew 21.31 = Mark 12.6 = Luke 20.13; Luke 18.2, 4; Hebrews 12.9). But its usage in the Apostolic Fathers shows that it can extend to respect for equals as well: *Hermas Vision* 1, 1, 7 respects as for a sister; Ignatius, *Ep to Mag* 6, 2, "pay reverence to one another."

[25] Wives must to show respect for their husbands through godly lives. Man, who was created first, is to have authority over his wife (see 1 Tim. 2:11-14). The wife was made out of his body (Genesis 2:21-24) to be his helper and companion (Genesis 2:20).

[26] The word 'United' in the New International Version. 'Cleave' unto his wife in the Thompson Chain-reference bible, Authorised King James Version. Three important words mentioned in Genesis by God are the following- Leave, Cleave and Become one flesh.

5

Leaving

Coming together is a beginning;
keeping together is progress; working together is success

Henry Ford

There are many significant components essential for a stable, meaningful and healthy marriage. God-ordained marriage is never intended to be a one-sided affair. It takes two partners jointly working and walking together as a team for a successful, and long-lasting marriage. If one spouse arbitrarily controls the marriage while neglecting the other, the intended life-long, meaningful, happy and healthy marriage will be miserable and end up in failure.

The ideology of 'leaving' in marriage is first cited in the book of Genesis 2:24, "… a man will leave his father and mother and united to his wife." Let us look at what is meant by 'leaving.' It simply means that all less important relationships must give way to the newly formed marital relationship, which is more important in life than anything else.

'Leaving' is not an easy choice but the best choice one may ever have to make in marital life. Entering into a marital life is a firm commitment between the spouses and with the Almighty God. Leaving signifies going through life together 'for better or for worse.' However, there are times it becomes apparent that it is not in the best interest of either party to stay married as they feel that they have tried every attempt for reconciliation, and it has not worked. Without leaving, cleaving and weaving is impossible for a successful marriage.

There are two types of the act of leaving in every marriage. First, it is a public act, which means that the bride leaves her home where she was born and joins the bridegroom's home. Second, it is a legal act. The exchange of vows during the marriage ceremony, and the act of being proclaimed as husband and wife confirms it. They affix their signature in the church register in the presence of the church assembly and above all in the presence of the Almighty.

God instructs the importance of 'leaving' in the very first marriage recorded in Genesis 2:23-24. " … a man will leave his father and mother and be united to his wife." God considered its significance, even though Adam did not have a parent. God addresses the husband first because he is considered as the head or the leader of the home. He cannot lead a successful home if he is still emotionally living with his parents. Therefore, according to God's plan, he must leave his parents emotionally in order to lead a brand-new home efficiently, effectively and successfully for God's glory.

There are primarily two types of relationships in the process of leaving. They are the parent-child relationship which is a temporary and secondly the husband-wife relationship which is the permanent one. "… what God has joined together, let man not separate" (Matthew 19:6). Therefore, the husband and wife call for a move from parent-child relationship to husband- wife relationship. This transition is necessary and important to have a healthy relationship.

Problems will precipitate in any family life when the parent-child or husband-wife relationship roles are reversed and the parent-child relationship is treated as the most important relationship instead of husband-wife relationship in marriage. When an adult child has married and this parent-child relationship remains as the primary relationship, the newly formed merger will not last and is always under severe stress. There are lifelong questions regarding its stability.

The Principles of Leaving

'Leaving' means that all lesser relationships must give way to the newly formed marital relationship, which is considered as a call to a personal family life. A leaving must occur to cement a covenant relationship of husband and wife. This principle of leaving applies likewise to our covenant relationship with God which is also seen in the life of disciples in relationship with Jesus, "… left everything and followed him" (Luke 5:11, 28; Mark 1:18). All these incidents show us that disciples left their old relationship, net and boat, for a new relationship with Jesus. They understood that new relationship, a close-knit fellowship with their Master and Saviour, is more important relationship than the old. There is nothing wrong to applying this principle in our marital relationship. In the marital relationship, one must have a close-knit fellowship and relationship, and then they will be able to leave their earlier pattern of life with their parents. Marriage is also a divine call for team work, 'until death'.

Generally, leaving someone or something is always a difficult thing to do. It is often hard for a foetus to leave its mother's womb, a comfort zone for ten months to a new different and unfamiliar zone. It may be considered to be cruel for a nurse or doctor to cut the umbilical cord, which binds the baby to the mother. Yet, it is necessary for the growth and development of the baby to disconnect from her / his mother's umbilical cord. It is also hard for children to leave their parents and for parents to let their children go. Just as babies cannot grow physically unless they leave their mother's womb and just as children cannot receive an education unless they leave home to go to school, a marriage cannot mature unless both partners are willing to leave their parents in order to cement a new marital relationship and establish a new family life. Therefore, for spiritual, emotional growth and development, there must be leaving which is essential and mandatory.

Who and what do we need to leave? Some of the major things we need to leave are our beloved parents, close friends, extended family, pets, sports, hobby, regular activities, regular television serials and selfish ways. Then the next question arises to our mind, how do we leave? We need to leave every aspect geographically, physically, emotionally, financially, and socially.

Aspects of Leaving
The Hebrew word *Azah* means to relinquish, loosen, forsake, leave, lose or discard. One must surrender the earlier arrangement or commitment, devotion to the father and mother, relinquish from it, and transfer the same to the spouse. Marriage calls for discarding all the previous affairs or relationships and give more priority to the spouse. If one cannot leave all other old relationships (emotionally, economically, psychologically, physically, and spiritually) they will not be able to leave and cleave to the spouse, and therefore there will be no stability in the marriage. This is not an advice to forget all the old relationships, but it encourages giving more priority to your spouse.

The Greek word *Kataleipo* which means to abandon, leave behind, have remaining. The role of father and mother: father, the principal or chief person in your life, and mother, the one who binds the family together, to leave from the old traditional mind-sets that you derived from your previous relationship to a brand-new relationship.

Leaving Parents

There are men and women who are unsuccessful in building a strong covenant marriage, due to various reasons. They are still 'tied to their parents,' or they are not willing 'to leave' their attachment to their parents, job, education, sports, past activities, friends, habitual methods or even church work, in order to establish strong marital relationships.

Leaving involves learning to dispose some of our parents' attitudes and influences. This is not always easy since we are largely the product of our upbringing. The process of adjustment to a new marital relationship requires that we learn to distinguish between what is fundamental and what is incidental to our past upbringing, being willing to leave behind the latter for the health and growth of our marriages.

Leaving involves not only leaving behind positions as dependent children, but also ending financial dependence from parents and slowly establishing their financial responsibility through their own income. The couple who never learns to stand financially on their own feet will have difficulty in developing their plans independently. Therefore, it is important to live within their own income, rather than be financially dependent on their parents. This does not mean the parents will not help their children. It only means that there should be growth from dependency to independency in financial matters also.

Married life involves leaving the intimate relationship with parents and looking forward to a new permanent relationship with the spouse with advice, help and guidance of the parents. This is a transition from psychological intimacy from the parents to the spouse. It may be difficult, but it is something that is required for a successful marriage.

Therefore, what is meant by leaving? Leaves means that you leave the dependence, comfort, and security of your parents' authority, breaking apart the old parent-child relationship, separating from your siblings and extended family to husband-wife relationship. This does not mean that you are cutting ties with dear parents or siblings, instead, you are forging a new relationship with them with your spouse.

Leaving means that you leave your parents in the area of decision making. You can turn to your parents for help, but any decisions must be made individually as couples. Leaving the parents does not mean to permanently withdraw and no longer have a healthy relationship with them. Desertion or isolation and leaving are two different things. Desertion or isolation is a permanent cutting off but leaving is temporary. We are not deserting our parents through our marriage; we are leaving the parents. Exodus 20:12, "Honour your father and your mother,"[1] means that when you leave your parents you must still show respect, love, admire, appreciate, show gratefulness and affirmation for their sacrifices and efforts to raise you as Godly child. "...so that you may live long and that it may go well with you in the land...." (Deuteronomy 5:16). You can honour the parents and reap benefits by seeking their advice, wisdom when need arise.

When parents cling to their earlier lifestyle and do not let go of their children, there will always be feelings of inadequacy. By helping and overprotecting their children, they give them the message that they do not have confidence in them or in their abilities. It does take time and training to help children to leave. Parents have to start training children very early in life. They have to prepare and guide them into adulthood.

The first step in establishing a marriage covenant is leaving all other relationships behind, including the closest ones - father or mother. "For this reason, a man will leave his father and his mother...." (Genesis 2:24). Of course, leaving does not mean desertion of one's parents. Every spouse has the responsibility to honour the father and mother as taught by Jesus in Mark 7:10-13. We should not escape our responsibility toward our parents especially when they grow older or become sick. Jesus scorned the hypocrisy of those who gave to the temple the money they had set aside for their parents (Mark 7:9-13). As adults, however, we assume responsibility for our parents rather than to them. The Bible never suggests that married couples should abandon their ties with their parents, but that they must let go of their former lives as sons and daughters in order to cement their relationships as husbands and wives. That does not mean we are neglecting or showing disrespect to our parents.

How do we honour our parents? Honour means value more highly than anything else - show respect, love, affection and care. Without these elements one cannot genuinely honour our parents. Leviticus 19:3 says, "Each of you must respect his mother and father." Firstly, recognize and give importance to their position as parents. One should show respect with their words, deeds and action privately and publicly. Secondly, adoring and loving them as parents. The word honour means to appreciate and value as precious people. Honour goes beyond simple respect for position and extends to the heart. Proverbs 31:28 says, "Her children arise and call her blessed; her husband also, and he praises her..." The very last verse of the Old Testament says, "...He will turn the hearts of the fathers to their children, and the hearts of the children to their fathers; or else I will come and strike the land with a curse" (Malachi 4:6). Thirdly, submitting to their authority. In the gospel of Luke, twelve-year-old Jesus went down to Nazareth with his parents and "was obedient to them" (Luke 2:51). Ephesians 6:1 says, "Children, obey your parents in the Lord, for this is right." Fourthly, to show acceptance and to be open-minded to their authority. Solomon gives adequate wisdom by saying, "listen, my son, to your father's instruction and do not forsake your mother's teaching. They will be a garland to grace your head and a chain to adorn your neck" (Proverbs 1:8-9).

Leaving Friends

Leaving the association of old friends and starting a new group of friends together in the new locality of their choice is necessary. This does not mean they are completely forsaking old relationships. Without neglecting the old, successful married couples start new friendships and associations.

You will need to shift the priority of your friendships, separate from past romantic and opposite-sex relationships, and leave behind your single lifestyle.

Leaving past romantic relationship with the opposite-sex does not mean that they ignore people; instead, they do not cherish and nurture those friendships due to new life long relationship.

Leaving Old Life Style

Leaving one's old lifestyle to a collective new lifestyle is necessary. Both adults must be prepared to leave individually and collectively many things in their life - how to utilize the free time, time to get up and time to go to bed, time to spend in quiet time and prayer time, time to spend with friends, and time to leave the home physically, relationally, emotionally, financially, spiritually and sometimes geographically.

Physically

Two or more members in the family living under one roof has its challenges. If possible, start living separately with your spouse as a tangible expression of leaving and cleaving. Leave home relationally. Marriage requires new priorities in life, most preference given to your spouse and nobody else. Parents are no longer your top priority in your new relationship, but it is your spouse. The wife's cooking is now your favourite food and the husband's achievement is to be admired.

Emotionally

Perhaps the most difficult possessions to leave behind are the inner wounds and hurts of our childhood and young days. We come to our marriages with both good and bad emotional experiences of the first few decades of our lives. Through the healing power of the Holy Spirit, we can be delivered from past wounds that can infect marital relationships. The love of Jesus and the encouragement and prayer support of our spouse can set us free from our past and enable us to be the understanding partner God wants us to be.

Good news or any achievement at work is first shared with the spouse and not with your parent. If you need to take a decision, talk it through with your spouse before approaching the parents. Have you left behind your parent's emotional control over your life? Do you ever look to them for emotional support, encouragement, decision making and any type of approval? Nothing wrong, it's natural. It's good to hear from your parents that they are proud of you. You may therefore long for it but you can no longer be dependent on it.

Husbands and wives must reorient their lives from the family of origin to the new family they are forming. One's spouse and children take centre stage; one's parents and siblings become peripheral by comparison. Some marriage partners fail to leave home, at least emotionally and mentally. This disorientation weakens their marriage.

Financially

It's time to give up the dependency on finance from parents. One of the greatest mistakes the young married couples make is wanting to have everything within a short span. Work hard, give graciously and generously, save diligently and then spend happily.

Spiritually

Being raised in a Christian home and going to church throughout the whole life does not make you a Christian. Personal faith in Christ alone leads to salvation and spiritual maturity in your life. Family heritage does not bring you into a right relationship with God. Have regular family prayer, study bible together, and have fellowship with your spouse.

Spirituality is a very important part of your impending marriage. If both of you are non-believers or from different denomination, now is the best time to talk through those issues. There is nothing more heart breaking than believing ahead of time that you will be likeminded spiritually only to find out that after the wedding vows one spouse has a completely different viewpoint than the other. Talk through all issues, include traditions, biblical interpretations, biblical translations, church attendance habits, prayer habits, Bible study habits, and any other issue important to you.

Geographically

There is nothing wrong when you move away and live separately from your parents. Leave peacefully and prayerfully with the blessings of the parents. This leaving helps to have more freedom to cleave and weave. Parents may visit once in a while.

It means leaving the home of the parents where you were raised and establishing a new home under the leadership of the husband in a nearby area or strange unknown place or even a foreign country under different circumstances.

A marriage is the union of two different families for good. Each partner brings different experiences, different insights, and different ways of living together into the new household. This will bring a fresh new start. The cross-fertilization of family cultures helps the human community prosper. As the human community grows, it requires a continual reshuffle of family commitments and human ties.

Have you noticed the parents crying when their children leave? Yes, it is painful, but they are confident that the married couple are going to leave happily. Long years of association with the parent-child relationship is breaking for a brand-new husband and wife attachment. If you have wonderful, loving parents, the idea of leaving them to get married may be very difficult as you've depended on them for security and companionship. The most difficult aspect of this leaving is emotional.

The leaving, however difficult it is, an inherent part of marriage. If the parents do not accept it, their children will be very unhappy. Therefore, they must be willing to commit themselves to it even though their son or daughter might not have chosen the perfect spouse.

The truth is, you could move hundreds of miles from home and not leave and you could live next door and leave well. Leaving has a great deal to do with your attitude toward and your dependency on your parents. Leaving means they are no longer the ones you go to when you are faced with problems. It means you don't depend on them emotionally, financially, or relationally. It means what they want or expect does not take priority over your spouse's wishes. It means you don't run to them when you and your spouse have a problem. Too often a young husband or wife will report every problem to one or both parents and do long term damage to the relationship between the parents and their spouse. Unless there is abuse, wise parents will encourage their married children to communicate with and work out problems with their spouses, instead of complaining to mom and dad. If counsel is needed, it's usually wiser to go to a pastor or counsellor who is not emotionally involved, and who can give biblical advice.

Leaving, also, means anticipating changes in family traditions. Just because mom and dad always celebrated Christmas at midnight on Christmas Eve, doesn't mean that's the way it has to be or, even, should be for a new family. This is one of those issues that can cause years of tears and anger. Couples should sit down and talk about these sensitive issues. Solutions will involve compromise, unselfishness, working together as a team, and the establishment of new family traditions. It may, also, require sitting down with one or both sets of parents and lovingly explaining your decisions.

Are you ready to leave the past behind to cleave to weave with your spouse?

Endnotes

[1] Ephesians 6:2; proverbs 30:17; Colossians 3:20; 2 Timothy 3:2.

6

Cleaving

Marriage is not a noun; it is a verb.
It isn't something you get. It's something you do.
It's the way you love your partner every day

Barbara De Angelis

Cleaving is the second essential component of a marriage covenant, "Therefore a man leaves his father and mother and cleaves to his wife" (Genesis 2:24). 'Cleaving,' reflects the central concept of covenant-fidelity. The Hebrew word for cleave is *dabaq*, which suggests that the idea of being permanently glued or joined together to something or someone. Similarly, after marriage a man is to pursue with diligence after his wife (the courtship should not end with the wedding vows) and he is to be stuck to her like glue. This cleaving indicates that there should be no other closer relationship.

Cleaving involves two key components, namely creating a marital identity and developing a bonding to your spouse. Due to lack of oneness, marriage suffers as one or both spouses remain more devoted to self than to their marriage union.

Cleaving can take place only where the leaving process has already taken place. This process reveals divine wisdom. A man and a woman must leave all lesser old relationships for the purpose of cleaving to their spouse. That is, cementing their new relationship and establishing a new healthy home. It is one of the words frequently used to express the covenant commitment of the people to God, "Fear the Lord your God and serve him, hold fast to him…" (Deuteronomy 10:20; 11:22; 13:4; 30:20). In King James Version instead of *hold fast*, the term used is *cleave to him*. The word is used to describe Ruth's refusal to leave her mother-in-law Naomi, "…but Ruth clung to her" (Ruth 1:14 New International Version). Ruth *cleave* unto Naomi (Ruth 1:14 King James Version)." From this verse, it is very clear that Ruth's loyalty and selfless devotion to her mother- in- law is very predominant. This must be the same attitude of the spouses in the marital relationship. Cleaving involves the whole hearted commitment, unwavering and unshakable loyalty towards one's marital partner. The man is to cleave to his wife only and nobody else from an old friendship. Cleaving to the spouse leaves out all marital betrayal and misbehaviour. A man or woman glued to their spouse cannot flirt, become unfaithful or engage in extra-marital relationships.

The word cleave also indicate not giving up when things go wrong, instead talk it out till clarified, expressing the spouse's opinion or feelings freely, willingness to rectify anything which hinders relationships, to ask pardon, take initiative in restoring confidence and the original commitment, to be transparent and reiterate oneness with the spouse. According to prophet Jeremiah cleaving means willingness to show submissiveness to leadership. Therefore, we should honour, respect, love, and serve the other person with an enthusiastic heart. Praise the spouse and build their

self-esteem day by day. In addition, when there is conflict, be quick
to admit faults and work out the differences in a Godly manner.

Cleaving means that our children or parents are secondary to
the spouse, even though they rightfully require much of our time
and attention to meet their needs. The husband and wife's unity
and oneness cannot be forfeited and the spouse's relationship with
one another is one of highest priority. When a husband and wife
cleave together, it means that they are now one and no longer two
individuals. Everything they do, whether positive or negative, will
affect the other.

The husband and wife are directed to cleave to one another.
Cleaving means, to stick together in their opinion, outlook, mind-
set, way of life, hopes, decisions, policy, and way of thinking and
going forward with oneness and harmony. The term cleaving denotes
leaving the old relationship, bonding with their new relationship and
establishing a new home with wholehearted commitment, which
glues them for a permanent relationship. Cleaving also indicates
willingness for change. Cleaving does not happen automatically: it
will take time and energy. It takes a remarkable amount of planning,
preparation, and hard work. You need to start thinking about cleaving
and you cannot do that if you are still in the process of leaving.

Seven steps to cleaving according to Dr. Bruce Wilkinson are:

- Leave everyone else completely, including old friends of
  the opposite sex.

- Remain pure sexually, this includes pornography.

- Love for the long term ... till death do you part ... no turning
  back no matter what ... splitting not an option. Think of
  the two of you in a boat 3000 miles at sea. If a problem

develops only option is to deal with it. You cannot swim to shore or jump ship.

- Live at your standard of living and not your parents or someone else's, learn the secret of being content and spending wisely, debt is a monster and Satan loves to use it as a tool.

- Work at marital happiness ... Love languages...serving ... romance ... more later.

- Forgive each other 70 times 70. Almost all affairs stem from unforgiveness causing a root of bitterness and a hardened heart.

- Keep God in the centre of your marriage. Let not man / woman, or children, or parents, or business, or friends or anything but God be with you as you allow him to mould you into one flesh.[1]

Cleaving demands an unconditional commitment, which spills over to every area of a spousal relationship. It means to be permanently glued together rather than temporarily taped or pasted together. We can separate two pieces of paper taped together, but one cannot separate, without great damage, two pieces of paper that are glued together. In fact, two pieces of paper glued together become not only inseparable, but also much stronger.

In a marriage covenant, cleaving does not allow the spouse to forsake the other even though the relationship is no longer satisfying. If the freedom to leave is retained as a real option, it will hinder the total effort of developing a marital relationship characterized by covenant faithfulness. Marriage counsellor Ed Wheat, observes an important fundamental fact about proper understanding of a marriage, "Keeping divorce as an escape clause indicates a flaw in your commitment to each other, even as a tiny crack that can be fatally widened by the many forces working to destroy homes and families."[2]

Dabaq (Hebrew) means to cling, cleave, stay locked, glue. *Kollao* (Greek) to join, to glue, means a bond between husband and wife for a healthy togetherness and intimacy in the marriage. Intimacy in a marriage relationship cannot be maintained without the proper understanding of the concept of leaving and cleaving. Intimacy requires the time spent with each other both in quantity and quality which will enrich the marriage, a steady and regular healthy communication, a time of exposure of inner thoughts, feelings and sharing of heart to heart persistently. In the quality or quantity of time, one must give undivided attention. Avoid crowded activities and try to spend time with the spouse. Couples need to share with each other and get to know each other's likes and dislikes. Couples need a time for both to mutually share without distraction from other people. A healthy conversation means active listening and it is essential not to let your eyes wander. So, the same way, eating in restaurant together, travelling together, and playing indoor or outdoor games together is essential.

Cleaving is the pursuit of common objectives in marriage that eliminate any tendency towards divergent operations and self-sufficiency.

Cleaving must have a Common Vision

This implies having a sense of belonging to each other in having a common vision, goal, and purpose in marriage. Marriage as a joint endeavour basically operates as a single venture and not as two separate enterprises under the same roof, which unfortunately in most marriages are a reality.

Fulfilment in marriage will only come out as a result of carrying out the scriptural injunctions on marriage and not just by marrying a particular individual. Therefore, a couple is expected to speak with a single voice. This means oneness of opinion rather than bargaining and arguments all the time. We all think differently. Where there is unity; there can be friction. However, to be able to speak with one voice requires submissive spirit. Submission in love, care and respect is what is required and not submission to an autocrat. There can only be one driver in a car. So, if both husband and wife are going to drive the same car at the same time, it will lead to a collision and cause great tragedy. This principle can be adopted in marital life also. Therefore, when two individuals speak with one voice and act with genuine unity, the marriage is on the right track. Many couples seem to get the wrong impression about submission and many women refuse to accept the idea of submission due to a wrong understanding of submission as suppression or enslavement to her husband. It is not so when it is understood rightly. On the other hand, the Bible teaches that partners in marriage should submit to one another. A common vision can be a sign of joint child rearing, nurturing, and discipline.

Being Transparent in all Possessions
This requires that the couple operate a joint financial arrangement in operations and belongings. A spouse is expected to inform or share his or her incomes, assets, liabilities and other financial obligations with the other spouse in the true spirit of oneness and transparency for a healthy and long-lasting relationship. This is not feasible where there is fear of sharing and revealing, or if they lack mutual trust, commitment and confidence in each other. Having joint possessions in marriage suggests that the couple have joint ownership of properties and investments such as lands and businesses. They must have knowledge about each other's investments, bank accounts

and all dealings in their marital relationships. Many couples hide from each other the true details of their finances, property, and different types of investments. This is an unsafe issue if one of the partners meets with sudden accident or death or goes through terminal illness and the other partner finds it difficult to sort out the details of their investment. These are rebellious, unethical, unbiblical and selfish attitudes that run contrary to the marital vows they took before God and his assembly to share everything together – 'I am yours, and you are mine.' Further, independent financial operations in marriage are contrary to the biblical principles of true companionship, stewardship, accountability, and transparency in marriage. A wife should be fully secure in the hands of a caring and loving husband.

The first two factors, namely, leaving and cleaving, are not fully and practically accomplished in many families in our society. In the Indian family, it is the patriarchal and patrilineal family that prevents couples from leaving and cleaving completely from their family ties. If leaving and cleaving factors of marriage are not fully accomplished, there are possibilities of misunderstandings, doubts, adjustment problems, harassment, interference of others and strained relationships.

Cleaving confirms the whole hearted commitment from both partners. There should be an unwavering loyalty and faithfulness towards each other. This will help them to stay away from marital unfaithfulness, misunderstanding, miscommunications, and ill-treatments of all sorts.

What is really meant by the old-fashioned term 'cleaving unto'? In the first place I think that it points to the warm and intimate closeness to each other. It is a matter of two people having to live very closely to each other. (A double banana looks like two but is in reality only one.) There is more to it, though. In the Bible 'cleave unto' also indicates that a dependent takes refuge in a stronger one (like Israel does unto God). The man and the woman are interdependent on each other. In the original Hebrew this points especially at strong love or committed, unbreachable pledge. It means reliability, genuineness, honesty, integrity, and fidelity.

If one is going to get married, it does not in the first place - as already said - mean that one now has legal rights to the other's body. Marriage means that troth is promised to each other in public. And however old-fashioned the Bible and the marriage formulary might sound - this is a promise for a lifetime. Only death can bring an end to it.

Of the three words, leave, cleave unto and being one, the middle is the most important, as it uncovers the deepest mystery of marriage. The leaving might be imperfect, and the unity, being one can fail, but if you do not cling to each other in troth, your marriage will inevitably be doomed.

It is wonderful to be in love with each other, and as you know it is not difficult, as it practically falls into your lap like a gift. However, to remain in love takes effort, it is a duty. At times the wife - for the sake of peace and love - must be willing to pick up her husband's clothes from the floor. At times the husband will have to have infinite patience with his wife because she is 'crying for nothing' again - simply because he loves her.

When Genesis 2:23-24 refers to cleaving, it is the idea of becoming one flesh with your spouse. Sexual intimacy is the culmination of the leaving and weaving process. Therefore, it is the pinnacle of intimacy that assumes true leaving and cleaving. In God's perfect design, you have to leave and weave before you can become one flesh. If you continue to value affection from other people more than affection from your spouse, or if you continue to hold back parts of yourself from your marriage, you will never experience the unity and oneness that God designed marriage to contain.

Most often, when sexual problems arise in a marriage, people assume they are either incompatible or that one partner has issues with their sex drive. While preferences and drive to play a role, sexual problems are usually indicators of a deeper concern within the relationship. It's possible to have sex without biblical, 'one flesh' unity, as an angry couple can have sex, but it is not one-flesh intimacy. The physical act happens, and a type of physical satisfaction may be experienced, but the spouses do not experience the same type of glory that is experienced when sexual intercourse is the result of a strong marriage based on leaving and weaving.

The word that the King James Version translates as cleave is translated elsewhere as 'join,' 'cling,' or 'unite.' I like the term cleave: it sounds like a bond with the strength of super-glue. At least in part, this is a sexual image. In sexual intimacy, a husband is physically joined to his wife. "The man and his wife were both naked, and they felt no shame" (Genesis 2:25).

The union of a husband and wife is a cleaving in every sense: emotionally, socially, economically and spiritually. It is intended to be an enduring, in-dissolvable union. This intent is captured in the wedding vows, in which a husband and a wife promise to remain faithfully united to each other "for better or for worse, for richer or for poorer, in sickness and in health … until death do us part."

Cleaving is both a commitment and a process. It's a commitment in that it requires a firm decision on the part of both partners to stay together through thick and thin. We vow to be true to our spouse through arguments, annoyances, differences of opinion, having children, losing children, changing jobs, moving to new cities, times of physical separation, mid-life crisis, changes in appearance, becoming attracted to someone else, growing old, growing sick, and whatever else life throws at us. Cleaving requires both the husband and wife to stubbornly hold on to the commitments they've made. Cleaving, however, is not just a matter of the will. Time and experience actually strengthen the union between husband and wife.

When I asked few couples what helped them physically cleave to one another after getting married, the top response was geographical distance between the couple and extended family. For some people this was merely a matter of doing what we've already talked about – taking time away from extended family in order to strengthen the brand new marital bond between the two. Physical distance from extended family during this initial stage of marriage causes the following benefits, all of which help develop the cleaving time. You will need one another for daily support. Knowing that when you get back together with extended family you can share experiences and bond over again to reconnect.

Spend as much time as possible talking together, praying together, walking together, getting to know each other as husband and wife. Also learn to keep personal issues between you and your spouse. This is the beauty of cleaving. One can cleave spiritually by praying for each other, praying together, attending Church together, participating in Holy Communion together, attending the church activities together, participating in missionary activities together and giving alms for the poor and needy. This is a perfect example of spiritual cleaving.

Endnotes

[1] Bruce Wilkinson says in his twenty five plus years of counselling he has come to the conclusion that just about every marriage problem he has encountered has been the result of one or the other partners in a marriage being in violation of what he considers the most important verse in the Bible as it relates to marriage. That verse is found in Genesis 2:24, which says: For this cause a man shall leave his father and mother and shall cleave to his wife and they shall become one flesh.

[2] Ed Wheat & Gloria Oakes Perkin, *Love Life for Every Married Couple: How to fall in love, Stay in love, Rekindle your love,* Zondervan, Grand Rapids:, Michigan, 1980.

7

Weaving

Marriage, like a submarine,
is only safe if you get all the way inside

Frank Pittman

The third essential ingredient of a marriage covenant is that "….they become one flesh" (Genesis 2:24). 'Weaving' is a textile terminology which is borrowed here for 'one flesh' concept. Weaving is a method of textile production in which two distinct sets of yarns or threads are interlaced at right angles to form a fabric or cloth. The longitudinal threads are called the warp and the lateral threads are the weft. The way the warp and filling threads interlace with each other is called the weave."[1]

Weaving means united and together. A 'one flesh' experience is the exchange of imaginations, emotions, joint venture and oneness. It is knowing each other in a cherished way that can only be experienced in the sexual relationship within the marriage relationships without any anxiety. Sexual intimacy and fulfilment is a by-product of a healthy marriage relationship, it also symbolizes how a husband and wife become one. It also means that there is ample transparency and openness with one accord. Weaving or one flesh is the interaction of heart and expression through words. This will lead to conversation which will help them to make genuine love.

Weaving involves physical intimacy. "... I am fearfully and wonderfully made;..." (Psalm 139:14a). God the Father created the couples fearfully and wonderfully. God the Son who redeemed the bodies through his blood, "...you yourselves are God's temple and that God's spirit lives in you" (1 Corinthians 3:16). The weaving never happen on the wedding day or night or honeymoon period. It is the process very likely ever to be complete. It is a calling of Christian couples, a destination toward *until death* which they constantly and continually travel.

In the marital relationship, the experiences like past memories, achievements, failures, adventures, fights, and disagreements form an intricate knit that holds together in the relationship. In the book, *Intimate Allies*, the authors describe weaving as the intercourse of heart and word. It involves the making of stories in order to make love. Making stories is far more than sharing common experiences; it is much more than being together in a moment. Making stories is being transformed by the moment together.

How will you respond to challenges or trials in your marital life? Will you be quick and smart enough to take advantage of adversity to weave you tighter, or will you allow to tear you to many pieces? Weaving can be a hard work and needs, deliberate and constant effort. It requires speaking the truth in love and honesty.

The sexual act should be playful, spontaneous, free, joyful and complete bodily surrender to your spouse and the equally joyfully receiving your spouse. "...and they become one flesh" (Genesis 2:26). The book Song of Solomon does not hesitate to describe this physical attraction of man and woman. God himself created man to have sexual urges and wants mankind to enjoy it within the marriage.

The sexual union within marriage is very important. This is not the one and only union, however. If there is no unity among man and wife in many more aspects, and if their unity does not grow, then the sexual bond will also lose its efficiency in the coming days. Financially and economically there has to be unity. Everything has to be shared in poverty and luxury. There has to be emotional unity in joy and sorrow to be shared. Be thoughtful about each other, accept each other, open up to each other, and try to understand each other.

The most important facet of this unity is faith in God. This deepest unity in faith will carry the marriage through every possible crisis in the future. Interaction with God in prayer and Scripture reading will give your marriage the dimension of the deepest and most unbreakable and permanent unity. 'One flesh' is an image of both sexual and psychosocial intimacy. A husband and wife are not only one flesh in the marriage bed, but also marital unity goes far beyond that. A surgeon joins two pieces of bone together, the two pieces knit together over time and become one. Husbands and wives, too, become one flesh as they live their lives together.

Only those who are naked and not ashamed can truly be one flesh. Nakedness, in the marriage is not just the absence of clothing. In Genesis 2:25, "The man and his wife were both naked, and they felt no shame." This was the attitude of man and wife before they committed sin. Husbands and wives who are 'naked and not ashamed' are open and genuine with one another because they have grown to trust each other. 'One flesh' has also the implications about the exclusive nature of the unique relationship between a husband and wife. Children are produced by the physical and sexual union of husband and wife. There is no coercion, manipulation or covering! You are united as one while remaining individuals, you are alike yet different. In marriage you are able to experience a mystery that has been reserved for those who dare to be naked and unashamed.

Weaving, what God calls a one flesh relationship, involves much more than a physical relationship, and sexual relationship (1 Cor. 7:3-5). This gives an assurance to show the divine intention for husband and wife. The sequence of marriage ingredients are leaving, cleaving, and becoming one flesh. H. C. Leupold explains that *becoming one flesh* "involves the complete identification of one personality with the other in a community of interests and pursuits, a union consummated in intercourse."[2] Couples who have been married start to think, act, behave and feel as one; they become one in mind, heart and spirit. The old chorus sings like this 'We are one in the spirit; we are one in the Lord.' So each couple has a spirit of oneness, one accord and one Lord.

As husband and wife leave other relationships and learn to cleave to one another, they become a new entity named as 'one flesh.' The phrase 'one flesh' needs some explanation because it is frequently misunderstood to refer primarily to the sexual union. The phrase is closely parallel to our English compound word everybody rather, we mean every person. Or when God speaks of destroying all flesh (Genesis 6:17; 7:21), obviously he does not mean all the flesh without the bones, but every person. Similarly, to become 'one flesh' (Genesis 2:24) means to become one operational unit. The phrase 'one flesh' needs some amplification so as not to misunderstand it to refer primarily to the sexual union.

But 'one flesh' is more than sexual union. It also means the oneness of the relationship between man and woman at a deeper level. The sexual union is a symbol of that deeper unity and also helps towards that bond.

The term 'one flesh' means that just as our bodies are one whole entity and cannot be divided into pieces and still is a whole, God intended it to be with the marriage relationship. There are no longer two individuals, but now there is one unit, a married couple. Through this new union, they become emotionally, spiritually, intellectually, financially, and socially one. Physically, they become one flesh. As a result of that, one flesh is found in the children that their union produces; these children now possess a special genetic makeup, specific to their union. This has two thoughts behind it. One is to be 'glued' to his wife, a picture of closeness through the marriage relationship. The other aspect is to 'pursue hard after' the wife. This is to go beyond the courtship and to continue throughout the marriage. The self-centeredness is the rut that marriages commonly fall into once the honeymoon is over. Self-centeredness has no place in biblical marriage.

It is in this spiritual union that two people are able to interpenetrate one another's life, and they become one flesh. Couples who have been married for many years start to think, act, and feel as one; they become one in mind, heart and spirit. The phrase 'one flesh' does refer to the physical or sexual aspect of marriage. The apostle Paul clearly uses the phrase in this way when speaking of sexual union between a man and a harlot (1 Corinthians 6:16). Sexual union does not automatically assure that a man and a woman become one in a mystical, emotional, and spiritual unity. Some men force woman for sexual relationship through rape or other immoral activities. This immoral activity cannot lead to the Biblical aspect of becoming one flesh. Sexual relationship without spiritual union of love, affection and mutual consent often leaves people separated, divided, guilty and bitter toward each other. The sexual objective must become the aspiration for the total blending and oneness of body, soul, and spirit between the marital partners. Therefore, any immoral sexual union itself does not bring about genuine oneness.

To achieve the biblical 'one flesh' union, sexual union in marriage must be natural as a fruit of love, affection, and care. If sex is not an expression of genuine love, respect, and commitment, then it is considered as a physical contact due to some pressure or conveniences while keeping the partners mentally and spiritually spaced out.

Sex is God designed; therefore it is good, exciting, fascinating, influential, and unifying. The Bible contains an inclusive 'theology of sexuality.' It contains the purpose of sex, clear cut warnings against its exploitation, and an attractive description of ideal physical intimacy as set forth in the Song of Songs. The 'one flesh' relationship (Genesis 2:24) is the most passionate, physical, spiritual and emotional unity between a husband and wife. God originally approves of 'one flesh' relationship (Proverbs 5:21) in which husband and wife meet each other's physical needs through sexual union (Proverbs 5:15, 18, 19). Paul indicates that sexual regulation in marriage can badly affect the Christian life, especially prayer life and daily walk with God. (1 Corinthians 7:5).

God gave the good gifts of sex. These are knowledge, comfort and satisfaction.

Knowledge "…with the help of the Lord I have brought forth a man" (Genesis 4:1). Here Eve acknowledged that God is the absolute source of life. Acts 17:25 states, "…he himself gives all men life and breath and everything else." Intimate oneness, the establishment of the new family unit Genesis 2:24,… "be united to his wife, and they will become one flesh."

Comfort, "….Isaac married Rebekah, she became his wife, and he loved her; and Isaac was comforted after his mother's death" (Genesis 24:67). It is meant to provide comfort to the spouse through marital relationships. The creation of life, for flourishing, filling the earth, to exercise dominion over other creatures (Genesis 1:28); for pleasure (Song 2:8-17; 4:1-16), and avoiding temptation (1 Corinthians 7:2-5).

Satisfaction- A husband is commanded to find satisfaction (Proverbs 5:19) and joy (Ecclesiastes 9:9) in his wife, and to concern himself with meeting her unique needs (Deuteronomy 24:5; 1 Pet. 3:7).[3] A wife's responsibilities includes availability (1 Corinthians 7:3-5); preparation and planning (Song 4:9ff); interest (Song 4:16; 5:2); and sensitivity to unique masculine needs (Genesis 24:67).[4]

God designed and created sex in marital life, to avoid all kinds of distorted behaviour, to avert all kinds of temptation like fornication, adultery, or extra marital sex by any one partner. The sexual relationship between husband and wife is a precious gift from God for the physical fulfilment and procreation of children. Physical intimacy between the husband and wife is good and holy in God's sight. But God puts restrictions on sex outside the marital relationship. The joy of the sex is not only a physical need but also an emotional and spiritual need. Without this intimacy, the closeness and oneness in marriage is not viable. Both have to blend to make it successful and joyful. In Hebrews 13:4, "Marriage should be honoured by all, and the marriage bed kept pure, for God will judge the adulterer and all the sexually immoral." Any kind of deceitful, dishonest, untrustworthy behaviour, impure thoughts or action should never come from the partners. Each partner must maintain faithfulness in their marital life.

Sexual union is a permanent and unbroken process. One of the disagreement between husbands and wives in every culture, in every faith mainly centres on the frequency of sexual relationships. Some wives complain that their husbands have nothing else in their mind, except thoughts on sex. Some others say that they do not enjoy sexual intimacy very often. There is no hard and fast rule set by anyone on the frequency of sexual relationship. This is a mutual need, which relies on the consent and decision of the partners. There could be many reasons for disagreements about frequency of sexual relations. Their reasons include that people are engaged with busy office schedule or other social activities; looking after the small children and in-laws, the elderly or the sick; physical and mental exhaustion after the work at the office or home; lack of interest or contentment, appropriate understanding about marital duties; less privacy at home; illness of anyone of the partner; a strong belief that sex is meant only for procreation and otherwise it is considered a sin; fear of pregnancy; different working hours for partners; fear of sexually transmitted diseases etc. Sexual union should be regular and should be a continuous process for a healthy marital life.

The apostle Paul in 1 Corinthians 7:3-5, outlines the basic principles concerning the satisfaction of sex in marital relationships. It is the marital duty, and fulfillment of basic needs of the partner. "The husband should fulfill his marital duty to his wife, and likewise the wife to her husband"(v3). Hence the couples cannot abstain from a sexual relationship. The couple must have regular sexual union, not for selfish desires, but for mutual satisfaction. It is marital authority that, "The wife's body does not belong to her alone but also to her husband. In the same way, the husband's body does not belong to him alone but also to his wife" (v4). This verse says that both of them have a marital right to fulfill and a special ownership towards each other. Once we get married, we are relinquishing the right to our own body, and share that authority with the other partner. This means that we must respect, love and care for our spouse's body more than ours. If we follow this biblical principle then there will be little place for abuse or ill-treatment in marital life. "Do not deprive each other except by mutual consent and for a time, so that you may devote yourselves to prayer. Then come together again so that Satan will not tempt you because of your lack of self-control" (v5). Some people have abnormal sex behaviour or drive, which causes abuse and ill treatment. This leads to rape within the marriage.

Aspects of Fulfilling the Duty

First and the foremost is the spiritual aspect. Both the husband and wife are raised in two different backgrounds therefore, their needs may be different. Both spouses might have practiced religion differently and their spiritual needs vary. Nevertheless, the abiding relationship with God is the most significant and imperative spiritual need. Uplifting, encouraging, edifying, and supporting each other is absolutely necessary. They need to maintain the spirit of Paul's command to 'bear one another's burdens' in the marriage.

Second is the physical aspect. Our basic physical needs are food, clothing and shelter. Failure to meet these needs results in marital problems. In the scriptures, the husband is commanded to provide or meet the needs of his family, while 'the wife of noble character' as mentioned in Proverbs 31 is to get ready to meet the needs. The husband is to seek the provision, the wife is to prepare for it. The husband is 'to bring or provides things,' the wife to 'serves it.' In yester years, husband was the breadwinner and wife looked after the children and cooked food for the family. The women did not receive much education and was homemaker. In contemporary times, both the husband and wife are employed; women are qualified, confident and are hired for higher positions. Many are forced to take the responsibility for the financial stability and smooth functioning of the family. Both of them have the functions of providing and preparing.

Third is the sexual aspect of the relationship. The apostle Paul advised the couple to 'fulfill their marital duty,' that is to meet the sexual needs of each spouse. Many couples have not experienced the joy of sex during their union due to lack of knowledge and understanding about sex or various other reasons. Sex is a precious gift of God for the purpose of reproduction, union and intimacy of the spouse. In addition, sex is interactive between the spouses for responding to each other's love.

Lastly, the emotional aspect of relationship. Each individual has different types of emotional needs. First and the foremost is affection. Every individual wants to know and feel that he or she is loved. Let the spouse feel that you love him or her with your personal care. Every person needs appreciation, acknowledgment and admiration for his or her achievements, or performances. It motivates the person to do better. In addition, most delightfully, it will change the attitude toward the partner. Giving an assurance or affirmation to the spouse for his or her approval, support, and encouragement is also necessary.

The Criteria for a Successful Sexual Relationship

For a woman, sexual feeling arises out of love and affection from the husband. She does not want to have sexual affair with a man who hurts her physically, emotionally, socially, or spiritually. She wants genuine love and affection from her spouse. For her, physical thirst will come only when she is emotionally one with him. Therefore, create an atmosphere for that oneness. But it is different for a man.

Trust and commitment needs to be built in order to have successful sex. It is important to trust each other in a marital relationships. The woman will not share her bed with a man who does not trust her completely.

Knowingly or unknowingly hurting each other physically, spiritually, socially and emotionally is not acceptable. Inner pain or wounds are more dangerous than outer pain or wounds. Inner hurting takes a longer time to heal than outer. Therefore spouses have to be careful in dealing with each other.

There are two types of guilt, namely true and false guilt. True guilt is positive in nature and false guilt is negative. False guilt can easily spoil a good marriage relationship. We need to, therefore, examine our marital relationships, to determine whether the guilt we feel over wrongdoing is true or false in nature.

Never cheat the partner by abstaining from regular sex. Due to ill health of a partner, abstaining from sexual relationship by the mutual consent for a brief time is understandable. However, one should never fool the mate by acting sick to avoid sexual intimacy.

Without any doubt one can say that loving, uplifting words can strengthen people and build strong inter-personal relationships. 'Talking' and more importantly, active listening to your spouse is an expression of your love towards your spouse. Without knowing your spouse, no effort can be made by the partner for change. Learn to manoeuvre around the 'triggers' that send your spouse into frustration and even anger. Be thoughtful and patient with the way you communicate; also be sure to recognize the way others receive information you send. Words can devour relationships. Speak easy and smile- it reflects good fortune and love.

Endnotes

[1] http://en.wikipedia.org/wiki/weaving (accessed on 24/01/2019).

[2] H. C. Leupold, *Exposition of Genesis, Volume 1* (Grand Rapids, Michigan: Baker Book House, 1979), 137.

[3] Daniel L Akin, *The beauty and blessings of the Christian bedroom*, Song of Solomon 4:1-5:1 (Englewood, New Jersey: Devora Publishing Company, 2003), 94-95.

[4] Ibid., 94-95.

Key to Closeness

*What greater things is there for two human souls than
to feel that they are joined... to strengthen each other...
to be at one with each other in silent unspeakable memories*

George Eliot

Communication

Communication is an indispensable part of human life. It is essential for a hale, healthy and happy wedded life. It is the exchanging of ideas, thoughts, opinions and sentimental feelings with each other. It is essential for the psychological, spiritual, social and physical growth of the individuals in the areas of abilities, skills, and intrapersonal capabilities. It also promotes the practice of interpersonal interaction.

Communication is defined as, "the sending out to someone an idea, feeling, or need in such a way that what the other person understands is reasonably identical to what you intended to say."[1] This definition explains that communication plays a great role in any healthy relationships. It will help us to realize who and what we are and what we know. Distorted communication leads to uncertainty, instability and confusion in relationships. An old proverb, "say what you mean and mean what you say," is commendable, but not easy to practice.

Another definition for communication is "a process by which information is exchanged between individuals through a common system of symbols, signs, or behavior."[2] This definition talks about verbal and non-verbal communication. The word 'listen' or 'active listening' is missing in this definition. Without active listening, there can be no genuine communication.

Communication "is the process of sharing yourself verbally and nonverbally with another person in such a way that both of you understand and accept what you say."[3] Some spouses have said that the longer they are married the less they need to talk about definite issues because they know each other's view so well. This may be true for some but not all couples. Getting to know each other is a long process. Some may achieve it in a short span of time and others may take a longer time.

The following are different types of communication. Examples of one way communication are lecturing; two way communication (discussion, feedback, and enquiry); non-verbal communication (body movements or position, facial expression, gestures, and postures); verbal communication (language is the chief vehicle for verbal communication); formal and informal communication (visual communication, telecommunication and through internet). All modes of communication are good in one way or another even in the marital relationship.

Biblical View of Communications

The apostle Paul in Ephesians 4:25-32 describes how communication should take place in our day to day life. "Therefore, each of you must put off falsehood and speak truthfully..." (v 25). When you've done wrong, admit it and when you are right praise God. Speak the truth in love to your spouse. Transparency must be maintained in our relationship with the spouse. There is no place for double talk in this beautiful and everlasting relationship (v 26). He emphasizes to keep your resentment, irritation, or anger under control. Anger is always a destructive force in marital life, inwardly and outwardly smashes the spirit of joy, peace and harmony in the family. He continues in (v 28) "...doing something useful with his own hands...". Each one is expected to say or do something useful, edifying and keep a cheerful personality. Don't reflect on problems only but always think of the solution and on the power of problem solving.

".....speak to men for their strengthening, encouragement and comfort" (1 Corinthians 14:3). The context for this passage according to the apostle Paul is exhorting prophesying in the church. He emphasized about strengthening, encouraging and comforting. Through our verbal and non-verbal conversations, we need to build, encourage and comfort each other. Use the words to build others, "...but only what is helpful for building others up according to their needs, that it may benefit those who listen" (Ephesians 4:29). God gives us the wisdom about our speech—Be Careful . . . Beware . . . so that we will be aware of the tongue's destructive power. But our speech can also be redemptive and full of grace, such a word is good for edification according to the need of the moment, so that it will give grace to those who hear it.

"Get rid of all bitterness, rage and anger, brawling and slander, along with every form of malice. Be kind and compassionate to one another forgiving each other, just as in Christ forgave you" (v31, 32). Forgiveness is the basic Christian attitude, which should be exhibited in our personal, corporate and family life.

The apostle Paul's advises, "Be very careful, then, how you live - not as unwise but as wise, making most of every opportunity..." (Ephesians 5:15, 16). Every spouse must draw a line between wisdom and foolishness. Foolish people does not make any plans, therefore they misses good opportunities. Wise people have proper planning; therefore they make use of every opportunity.

Make use of quality time for listening actively. "...everyone should be quick to listen, slow to speak, and slow to become angry..." (James 1:19). In order to understand more clearly active listening necessary. Listen wisely, cautiously, quickly to what the spouse wants to convey to you. Some spouses think that good communication always means agreement. Good communication need not end up with agreement. When you are in disagreement it is more likely that you are communicating well.

A timely advice is given by Solomon in Proverbs 15:23, "A man finds joy in giving an apt reply- and how good a timely word!" It is always meaningful, beneficial and edifying to say an apt word. Again Proverb 18:13, shed light to us "He who answers before listening—that is his folly and his shame."

Jesus' Model of Communication

Many of us might have attended seminars on communication but in reality we are struggling to communicate effectively in all areas of life. Jesus Christ, our role model, communicated his message to a wide variety of people, irrespective of their culture, creed, sex, behavioral pattern, and level of understanding. The method of Jesus' communication was to speak the truth with love, concern and care. Our Lord communicated in a way that combined the elements of teaching, inspiring, persuading, entertaining, correcting, rebuking, illustrating, questioning, encouraging, exhorting and listening actively.

God communicated to people in many different ways or methods. He never used only one style of communication. Jesus communicated according to the people's level. Our Lord knew how to proceed from a person's felt need to spiritual realities. Jesus knew how to target his message to his audience. In return, the people knew that the Good Shepherd was willing to lay down his life for his sheep. They never had to question his level of commitment, Jesus communicated truth that would stand the test of time.

Jesus' communication was creative. Our Lord never allowed his communication to become dull and boring. Jesus' communication was fresh, alive, interesting, dynamic and relevant to the particular gathering. Our Lord used this free flowing style of communication to build relationships that enhanced a two-way flow of information.

His communication was through eye contact. Some people's look is always threatening and intimidating, but Jesus always communicated with love, care, concern, compassion and understanding. Our Lord's visits made a great difference in the minds of people. His presence was an inspiration, he had a heart of acceptance, and he understood the people's condition and what they needed. Our Lord knew how to convey his message so that a transformation would take place in their thought pattern and behavior. He knew how to give effective feedback so that people could fully understand what he is saying.

Jesus used simple examples so that people could understand him. His examples were mostly of their day-to-day affairs, jobs, and other locally available things which could leave an impact on the people.

Jesus often used verbal and non-verbal communication in his public ministry. In fact, his spoken words were often substantiated by his actions. He touched and healed a leper, showing his compassion (Mark 1:40-45), with authority he drove the moneychangers from the temple, (Matthew 21:12-13). He washed the disciples' feet demonstrating servanthood, and taught his disciples to do the same (John 13:1-17). All of these actions were accompanied by words, but often his actions spoke louder than his words.

Effective Communication between Husband and Wife

Communication knits together spouses more closely. Good communication will remove all barriers and vacuum from their interpersonal relationships. Through sharing, a spouse can know what is going on in the other's mind, so that any misunderstanding can be dealt with quickly and efficiently.

When spouses talk with each other without any reservation, they get rid of negative feelings and avoid unnecessary misunderstandings. Keeping a verbal gap between spouses will only usher in disappointment, dissatisfaction, displeasure and insecurity. Healthy forms of communication are an antidote for all kinds of evil behavior. Communication in a marriage does not always take place verbally. Non-verbal communication includes facial expressions, hand signals, eye contact and body language. Ignoring non-verbal communication can drive two people apart or leave them feeling detached or isolated.

Open communication is like a road that always has a green light to give a signal to go forward without any disturbance. Good communication in a marriage allows the spouses to express themselves when they're in the mood for intimacy. Unsettled problems with physical intimacy can cause irreparable damages in the marriage in the long run. Good communication is vitally important for conflict resolution and for discovering causes of marital conflict. Good communication skills take time and hard work to develop, and even with ample practices there will still be times when it is very difficult to avoid confrontation. Ultimately, how you and your partner manage those situations is critical to the existence of your marriage.

Marriage can be nurtured into the joy that God anticipated for spouses. Good communication begins and ends with God who alone is the perfect, great and wonderful communicator. Therefore, marital life always need his redeeming involvement. We need to have a constant abiding relationship with him, which helps the spouses to have smooth communication. Be aware that there will be times of impulsive communication as well as planned communication in marriage. So be receptive to both of these. "A man finds joy in giving an apt answer — how good is a timely word (Proverbs 15:23)."

Communication is more than just words. It is the tone of voice, gestures, and body language. Do my words and body language go hand in hand? There is a common saying that actions speak louder than words. Specialists tell us that the majority of our communication is non-verbal. Timely, wise and edifying words are certainly important in good relationships, but the scripture also emphasize communication through our actions. The words normally and repeatedly used by spouses to each other, the way and the manner in which couples put their words together when they are angry or in normal situations can either affect them adversely or in a useful manner. Eye contact plays a prominent role in every communication. Never allow the eyes to wander during communication. At the same time, give undivided attention while speaking and listening to your spouse. While communicating, make it precise, specific, clear and understandable, and avoid rambling.

Take quality time for healthy communication. Lack of appropriate communication is the root cause for most relationship problems in a marriage. Spouses are busy with so many things in their lives that often they do not make time to spend with each other. Spouses who don't do so run the risk of having minor issues grow into major ones in a short span of time. Take quality time for the family - wife, children, parents, and in - laws. Get your priorities right. Prioritizing things is essential for marital life. Communication is not confined to speaking your feelings, but it involves the undivided attention of both parties.

In communication, listening plays a key role. Learning to listen and being willing to listen are the two essential elements in good communication. Listening to your spouse is about taking time to give your undivided attention, applying empathy and understanding what they really mean. Never assume anything and never pretend to be listening. Listen to the question and don't jump in too soon with an answer. In Proverbs 18:2 Solomon wisely put it this way, "A fool finds no pleasure in understanding….." Decide on a neutral time and place when both of you have time to relax, away from all routine work. Be totally open with each other. This can be during dinner time, in your living room or elsewhere. If you put off telling your partner what you need, it will chip away at your happiness and your bond.

Mark Twain said, "I can live for two months on a good compliment." His folksy wisdom is echoed in Biblical teachings about our words. "An anxious heart weighs a man down, but a kind word cheers him up" (Proverbs 12:25), "…your consolation brought joy to my soul." (Psalm 94:19), "A gentle answer turns away wrath…" (Proverbs 15:1). All these verses depict how kind words, consolation and gentle answers make a difference in our relationship with our spouse.

Edifying words are vital in all relationships, but is more significant in marriage. Begin with careful listening and allow time for your spouse to share his or her dreams, interests and fears. Get to know the thought patterns, feelings, desires, dreams, vision, and plans of your spouse as though they were your own. Develop an intimacy that is deeper than sexual relationship. Ask questions, and use what you learn in creative ways to encourage your spouse, shower compliments, have words of affirmation and during difficult times, bear each others' burdens through prayer.

Clarifying thoughts, ideas and plans that are ambiguous. Ambiguity means an idea, statement or expressions capable of being understood in more than one sense.

Be frank and honest in all your speech. Your spouse must know how and what you feel, and why you feel that way. Most women need meticulous information on day-to-day affairs whereas men prefer a speedy synopsis. Conversation must be simple. The spouse must understand what you are trying to say. Don't beat around the bush - just come out with what you have to say openly and transparently.

Good communication does not happen automatically or without any human intervention. Family life requires hard work from the beginning, first between the spouses and later as parent and children.

Ask yourself, 'Do I truthfully admire, trust, and respect my spouse?' Never disgrace or humiliate your spouse in front of others, especially in front of relatives, close friends or children. It only intensifies or invites troubles. Be honest, but also be kind. It is important to express your needs, but while doing so, one should not criticize your partner harshly or unduly.

Never utter any cursing or abusive names or words while having an argument. Too many marriages have been destroyed that way. The Bible tell us not to use any obscene or abusive language. The words will be an encouragement to those who hear them. Be aware of body language, tone and volume of voice. Communication includes the subtle ties of body language, tone and overall volume. Raising the voice indicates aggression, as does continually pointing your finger at your partner. In an emotional situation, it can sometimes be very difficult to moderate these behaviors, but that does not mean that you should not make the effort.

When spouses develop healthy communication and apply it in their marital relationship, the rewards will be far-reaching. It will certainly reduce marital conflict to a large degree, as well as internal discord and emotional pain. It increases mutual harmony and emotional stability. Although conversations about sex can be intimidating, they are worth discussing as there is nothing unholy, unethical and unbiblical in it. So if you are not getting what you need in the bedroom, don't despair and talk to your partner. It also results in a more rewarding sex life as it culminates to an increased sense of togetherness and the ability to receive pleasure from one another.

The accomplishment of closeness depends on good communication from both sides. When spouses are willing to share their feelings, thoughts and ideas without any fear of being misunderstood or suppressed in any way, chances are better to achieve stronger intimacy in their marital relationship. Every phase of one's life improves when you become a better communicator. Most conflicts begin to enter into the picture when we share our opinions, feelings, or needs. However, most successful relationships are those in which each person feels comfortable in sharing their feelings and needs. Communication is the cornerstone of any healthy relationship.

Communication in marriage can now and then slow down over time as you get to know each other better and more profoundly. Eventually there may not be as many things you don't know about each other as when you first met. Communication in marriage desperately needs to take place at times when couples are going through a rough patch in their marriage. In every marriage, the couple will come across complex issues and when it does, it should be sorted out at that time.

As couples continue to mature and their life style changes, a greater focus is required to improve their communication. Differences should always be acknowledged between the spouses and rejoice in the differences. There need not be a reason for resistance, as there is no wrong or right way to communicate. Taking time to understand your spouse can greatly improve the communication between the spouses.

Manage difficult conversations cautiously. Good and healthy communication is an ongoing process, but at the same time difficult conversations require special thought. Take time to think about what you want to say, and what you want the outcome to be, preparing yourself for the way in which you expect your partner to react. In many cases, difficult conversations are prompted by one partner, who is much better prepared than the other. Don't allow the conversations to become one-sided or manipulative. Know precisely what you want to talk about. You need to have clarity of thought in your mind. Let your spouse know what you want to discuss and then decide to have a common venue. The common place means a convenient place, a place where there will not be any disturbances from the children, in-laws or others. It should be a place where both spouses can concentrate. Try to reach a consensus as much as possible. That is good for both of you to maintain a spirit of oneness.

Barriers to Effective Communication

A barrier to communication is any complexity, obstacle, hurdle, or trouble which blocks the meaning and arrests the smooth flow of communication. Communication become ineffective, unsuccessful, and unproductive due to various reasons. King Solomon put it wisely by saying "Keep thy heart with all diligence; for out of it are the issues of life" (King James Version Proverbs 4:23), "A cheerful heart is good medicine, but a crushed spirit dries up the bones" (Proverbs 17:22)," 'Bitter hearts produce bitter words, joyful hearts creates joyful words, and loving hearts makes loving words.' This is a common saying, which is true in marital life.

What makes marital communication so intricate, or complicated? One's concept on communication in family life is mostly based on what is observed, heard or experienced as a child or an adult. For a few, their parents may have never properly communicated with each other or with their children. They may have told them that children are to be seen and not heard. They may have heard harsh words, or observed physical abuse followed by a simple conversation. Television serials, cinemas, internet, Facebook, WhatsApp, video games, computers, phones have taken over all our time, and it takes us away from those near and dear to us. We become comfortable finding our own meaning, purpose, and values without having to interact and communicate with others. Another barrier is work area pressures and other preoccupations which can steal quality time for communication between husbands and wives. We tend to be lazy, therefore we always find lame excuses to avoid confrontation or any difficult conversation.

When communication is only one-way, it becomes selfish or egocentric and it will unquestionably destroy any relationship. Personality struggles between spouses diminishes the ability to communicate properly.

Lack of self-confidence will lead to communication deterioration. As a result, spouses are afraid to communicate due to poor self image.

People today indulge in a multiplicity of communication tools such as telephone, mobile phone, e-mail, and WhatsApp, which lack certain basic components of inter -personal communication. In telephone conversions, normally there would be no body language visualized and tones cannot be understood, which can cause listeners on the other side to misinterpret the speakers' real meanings and which can cause cynical or amusing messages to seem intimidating.

Difference in perception is a major hindrance. This is mainly determined by the difference in age, nationality, religion, culture, education, occupation, sex, status, personality, and experience. Illiteracy, customs, beliefs, language and social class all play a significant role in communication. People from diverse cultures and religious backgrounds can experience complexity in understanding each other's outlook. Expert communicators overcome this barrier by using simpler and clear cut language.

A soft tone of voice will suggest that you are unsure of what you're saying. Whether it is verbal or non- verbal communication, ensure that your thoughts are well organized for better understanding. Organizing your thoughts is context-dependent, but it is always very important that your listener is able to follow the thought. Disorganized plans and conversations cause confusion to spouses, and will result in a lack of attention, and ultimately, a non-effective expression of ideas.

An inadequate understanding of a topic saps your authority and makes it difficult to build trustworthiness with your spouse. Inaccurate or a wrong use of a terminology detracts from credibility.

A feeling of disapproval or rejection is enough to cause some people to refrain from expressing themselves. Some people assume that they won't get their preferences, wants, and desires addressed because they are too frightened to express themselves in a specific language; therefore they beat around the bush. This is more likely to increase the chances of disagreement, and could end up in unpleasantness. Likewise being pessimistic in your approach puts your communication on the wrong foot. Learn to be positive.

An uncontrollable anger or a provoking manner of talk will lead to poor and unhealthy communication and also create a fearful and confused message in the life of the spouse.

Some people brand their spouse as irreversible, inflexible, useless, and old fashioned in front of others. This will only cause resentment and hostility. Reprimanding should only be done in the privacy of the home, with love and encouragement. We should never be envious or jealous towards our spouse. When one is doing a good job then appreciate it. There may be a quiet or silent partner. No proper and healthy communication is always silent. This is a poor communication method. Blaming one's spouse, pointing to him or her as the cause of problems in the family, should always be avoided. Consistent sarcasm in communication shuts out all other healthy communication. It demonstrates disrespect for another.

Selective listening includes listening to certain and wanted items of the spouse's communication and ignoring the rest of the message. Therefore, work on keeping the lines of communication open so that you can work through marital problems while they are minute, before they get devastating.

It is easy to start an argument or dispute by complaining or making a malicious or angry remark, setting the tone for a fight. Tell your spouse how you feel and what you wish he or she would do differently next time. Give your partner time and opportunity to explain what they were thinking and why they thought the behavior was appropriate. Placing blame is one of the biggest barriers to effective communication. Avoid barriers to effective communication by giving the spouse a chance to explain his or her side of the story and look for common ground.

Disagreeing and acting defensively while hearing the other person is to be discouraged. Defensiveness has a tendency to be a communication patterns which leads to arguments. It is the most frequent and harmful communication pattern between couples.

John Gottman identified criticism and defensiveness are as two key components in marriage that lead to separation and divorce. An automatic emotional reaction to condemnation is hard to resist. It is a type of defense mechanism. Dr. Gottman argues that "defensiveness is fundamentally an attempt to protect you and ward off a perceived attack."[4] When a spouse become defensive in marriage, they become closed off to the suggestions their spouse is providing. Gottman added, "The major problem with defensiveness is that it obstructs communication. Rather than understanding each other's perspective you spend your discussions defending yourselves. Nothing gets resolved, so the conflict continues to escalate."[5]

Secondly, defensiveness creates contention in all relationships. When defensiveness and contention are present, the conversation is usually over—at least the productive part. Defensiveness leaves the spouse feeling useless, inadequate, ineffective, or misunderstood.

Thirdly, defensiveness keeps the spouse from accepting the task or job. If a spouse is defensive, they are justifying their behavior, or blaming their partner for the problem. In essence, the defensive partner is telling their spouse, "The problem isn't me, it's you."[6]

Finally, defensiveness keeps husbands and wives from putting their spouse's needs and happiness above their own. In a sense, the defensive partner is saying, 'I don't care what you need in the marriage, this is what I need.' Defensiveness is self-focused. True love is when we focus on our partner's needs before our own. Gordon B. Hinckley advised couples, "If you will make your first concern the comfort, the well-being, and the happiness of your companion, sublimating any personal concern to that loftier goal, you will be happy, and your marriage will go on through eternity."[7]

Endnotes

[1] Grace H Ketterman, *Understanding your child's problems* (Grand Rapids, Michigan: Fleming H. Revel, 1992), 31.

[2] *Merriam Webster's Deluxe Dictionary* (1998), s.v. "communication."

[3] H. Norman Wright, *Communication: The Key to Your Marriage, The Secret to True Happiness* (Regal Books, 2012), 61-64.

[4] John Gottman, *Why Marriages Succeed or Fail – And how you can make yours lasts* (Simon & Schuster: New York, 1994), 85.

[5] *Ibid.,* 90.

[6] John M. Gottman, *The Seven Principles for making marriage work,* (New York: Three Rivers Press, 1999), 32.

[7] Gordon B. Hinckley, *The Teachings of Gordon B. Hinckley,* (Salt Lake City: Deseret Book, 1997), 329.

9

Basic Foundations of Marriage

The best time to love with your whole heart is always now,
in this moment, because no breath beyond
the current is promised

Fawn Weaver

Gone are the days of 'until death do us part' in marriage and also the distinction between man and woman. In the modern trend, marriage is no longer confined to male and female but today same gender marriages have become common. Apostle Paul, time and again, writes that they are deviated from the basic foundation of faith and a deviation from a call to holy living. Now many surround their life with popular views, emotions and social media responses, especially the total number of 'likes' they receive after they post a photo or some post on social media like Facebook, YouTube, Twitter, blogs, Instagram, LinkedIn, Pinterest, messenger, WhatsApp , Flip board etc.

In Psalm 11:3, the psalmist asks the question, "When the foundations are being destroyed, what can the righteous do?" Matthew 7:24-27 talks about the wise and foolish builders. The wise man built his house on the rock and the foolish man built on sand. Both wise and foolish man constructed the house on a foundation. But the quality of the foundation was different; one on rock and other on sand. The foundation on the rock could withstand drought, heavy rain, flood and wind. Therefore, those who enter into the marriage relationship must ensure that the foundation is built on Jesus Christ, our rock, shelter, fortress and refuge, "Unless the Lord builds the house, its builders labor is vain" (Psalm 127:1). It is our Lord who provides shelter and security for those who seek guidance and help. Therefore, we need to build our marriage and home with the help of God. Our abiding relationship with him, our dependency on his eternal word and our prayer life will carry the families through all winds, flood and rain throughout our life.

In the modern era, many young people live under the false impression that a marriage will work out automatically without any hard work and preparation. Therefore, they enter into the matrimony with a passionate feeling of sexual or sensual love. Their overwhelming sexual feeling for each other blinds them of the reality of what real marriage is. That is why we often hear, 'love is blind; marriage is the eye opener.' Love is a long sweet dream; marriage is the alarm clock. Wake up guys and girls! Facing reality in life with boldness is where 'true love' begins. There are plenty of challenges, struggles, painful experiences, and constant repair works. Someone once said "Marriage is like flies on a window panel, those from the outside want to get in, and those from inside want to get out." However, this is not true with every individual. Those who are committed and loyal to their partner, and experience true genuine love would happily stay in holy matrimony and not want to get out, even under difficult circumstances.

Here are a few strong pillars for marriage which are essential towards building a strong family life. A 'strong family' entails living a joyful, meaningful, and God honoring life 'until we are separated by death.'

The Pillar of Love

The following verses in the Bible clearly state the love defined by God. Love is a matter of choice, Colossians 3:14, "....binds them all together in perfect unity." Love will still be the governing principle that controls what the redeemed people do and how they behave. Love is a matter of conduct, we read in I John 3:18, " ...let us not love with words or tongue but with actions and in truth." The love of God pours into the hearts of the believers which in return enables the believers to love other fellow believers. Love is a matter of commitment, Romans 8:38-39, "...to separate us from the love of God that is in Christ Jesus our Lord." Love is a matter of covenant, Hebrew 13:5, "...Keep your lives free from the love of money and be content with what you have....".

Ephesians 5:28-30, "... husbands ought to love their own wives as their own bodies. He who loves his own wife loves himself ... just as Christ does the church - for we are members of his body." We can understand how to communicate love by thinking of the word LOVE.

Adapted from Edward Worthington's book, "*Hope Focused Marriage counselling.*"

L- Listen. How frequently do we listen to each other in our marital life? Genuine communication is a two-way system of a discourse and not a monologue. Actively listening to your spouse, then say again, what you heard and summarize your partner's thoughts and feelings. When you summarize, you confirm what you heard in order to avoid misunderstandings or lack of a proper response.

O - Observe. Look at the person you are talking to, 55% body language; 38% tone and 7% words. When you observe a reaction to what you are saying, clarify. Somebody rightly puts it like this,

"90% of the resistance and annoying of day-to-day life is caused through the wrong tone of voice."

V - Value. How do we value each other? Here the word 'value' means respect and accept each other as they are. This is the number one key for keeping communication flowing smoothly and therefore it reduces or resolves differences of opinion. Never degrade the partner, always uplift the partner.

E- Embrace. We need to embrace each partner constantly and each other in mutual love in seeking the best for each other. One of the goals of love is to build up, to enrich and empower each other. Ephesians 5:28-30 exhort us to nourish and cherish our spouse, just as Christ does to the church. The terms nourish and cherish are explained in previous chapters. When we encourage and give support to our spouse, we are empowering them to grow and develop their abilities and gifts. In this hostile world, our children and the generations to come are exposed to physical abuse more than physical embrace in marriages. The book titled *'Abuse of women in Indian Christian families-Roles of Clergymen, Church and Theological institutions'* by the author gives a detailed study of abuse. Why should we be ashamed to embrace our spouse? How often do you embrace your spouse? Romans 13:8 tell us to "…except the continuing debt to love one another, for he who loves his fellowman has fulfilled the law." We need to embrace our spouse not only physically but also spiritually, and emotionally.

The pillar of trust

Trust is the most important ingredient in any human relationship especially in a marital relationship. The more we trust, the deeper will be our relationship with each other. Trust means constant honor and care towards each another. Without mutual trust no relationship can survive. It is difficult to rebuild trust when confidence and our inter-personal relationship are rusted or broken. Today, a lot of marriage relationships break down because the simple component of trust has been broken.

Develop an appropriate level of trust before one becomes suspicious and obsessive jealousy. Trust levels need to be tested and recognized with practical aspects of the relationship, namely trust with finances, with children, secrets, inner family decisions and personal choices for better endeavors. In any healthy marriage relationship, when there is mutual trust, there is a greater level of transparency, accountability, love, care and stability.

The pillar of sexual union

The Bible clearly states that in marriage 'They become one flesh' (Genesis 2:24c; 1 Corinthians 6:16; Matthew 19:4-5). Two (man and woman) become one flesh. This is the expression which denotes the sexual union between man and woman. It is an activity of mutual consent of both husband and wife. Without a healthy sexual relation, there is no possibility of fulfillment in God-ordained marriage. There is nothing unholy, impure or unethical about the sexual union within the marriage. Sexual relationship outside the marriage will damage the relationship and is a gross perversion of the divinely established marriage union. Sexual union is not only a physical activity, but it is also a spiritual and emotional activity (1 Corinthians 6:15-29).

The pillar of intimacy

Intimacy is an intensely personal relationship of sustained closeness over time in which each partner is affectionately and unconditionally accepted by the other through congruent, empathic, conflict-resolving, self-disclosing, and distance-respecting mutual responsiveness. "The intimate relationship endures over time. To the degree that intimacy is not sustained over time it is less likely that the relationship will become and or remain healthy."[1]

The simplest meaning for intimacy is a feeling of understanding, closeness and attraction. It is noticeable by a very close connection, friendship, contact and familiarity. It is a significant element in any marriage. Each spouse must understand the need of intimacy of the other for the benefit of a smooth relationship in their marital life.

Spiritual intimacy
In having an intimate relationship with Christ, they experience the selfless and unconditional love of Christ. Through this intimacy they find freedom in Christ and experience the freedom in their marital life. They are also able to forgive each other and are filled with the peace of mind in themselves and with their spouse.

Physical intimacy
This is quite different from a sexual relationship. It entails a kind, caring, gentle and compassionate touch, a sincere hug, (not like the hug by Judas), pat, smile and a willingness to understand different body languages. Expressions like, 'I really appreciate you,' 'you are special to me,' 'you are always with me in my personal trouble' are extremely important. External expressions of affection are very important in a healthy marriage. Some spouses give less importance to this. For physical intimacy quality time is needed. Touching and patting leads to successful sexual relationships. Foreplay will help the spouse to have a gratifying sexual union. The sexual relationship between husband and wife is a reward from God for the gratification of physical intimacy and the procreation of life. In addition to procreation, God gave humans physical intimacy to enhance closeness and oneness within the marriage. The physical union of husband and wife is planned by God to plan a God-given aspiration for companionship, to protect the husband and wife from enticement, and for the mutual giving and receiving of great enjoyment and happiness between the husband and the wife.

Emotional intimacy

It is an emotional closeness, a collective sympathetic understanding and inclusive understanding of trust for each other. This experience can only occur between equals (human and human). For intimacy to exist, emotional closeness must flow to and fro. It must be give-and-take, and it can only exist by mutual consent. If one individual wants closeness and the other individual does not, then the relationship is not intimate.

People in a healthy intimate relationship tend not to feel the need to defend themselves. In a truly intimate relationship, it is extremely difficult for individuals to lie or hide the truth from one another. Body language tends to reveal the truth, and non-verbal signals go beyond all verbal concealments. Pornography and sexual infidelity has affected many marriages adversely more than ever before, and yes, Christians are no exceptions.

A close affinity with one's spouse in the bedroom is necessary. The spouse needs to know that her partner understands how he/she is feeling, what he/she is feeling, and why he / she is feeling it. The husband must be aware that women are generally more emotional than men. Therefore, he needs to be more sensitive. Wives mostly communicate through emotional feelings. The husband may not want to share the problem but it is important to resolve the problem by being sensitive to one another.

Sexual intimacy

It is the final stage of all the other intimacies. This will take place only when all other intimacy requirements are met adequately. Otherwise it is a routine, regular, and automatic exercise, merely a contractual obligation, marked by force and chores rather than by caring and meeting mutual needs and closeness. Sexual intimacy should be a normal and permanent part of their relationship.

Companionship through sexual intimacy is set aside for the husband and wife and individually designed to defend the husband and wife from inducement or enticement.

Everyone wants intimacy in their personal and marital life. In fact, a question remaining in people who find themselves alone is, 'How can I find intimacy with another person without the risk of giving up my individualism?'

Intimacy does not occur easily, and achieving intimacy seems to be a long process. Intimacy is an intense gift and being in an intimate relationship is a humbling experience. Intimacy enhances individual character in the midst of deepening inter-personal closeness. Without empathy a relationship has little chance of evolving in a healthy direction.

Intimacy is the quality of being close, and affectionate with another person. It is a close relationship in which two individuals, even when at a distance, are responsive to each other. A brief moment of strong, overjoyed closeness with another person must not give the wrong idea or indication of an intimate relationship. In intimacy, there is a shared, sustained relationship over time. Sex does not comprise intimacy; nor is it a healthy substitute for it. However, it can be a reaffirming enrichment of mutual intimacy. Couples in a truly intimate relationship tend to be comfortable with tactile or bodily closeness, and their emotional closeness becomes embodied in a high level of comfort with physical touch. In fact, a relationship may suffer without ecstatic moments. These moments can feed the roots of the relationship. While it is not a necessary condition, tactile intimacy may be, at times, the fitting expression of close companionship.

Intimacy reaches the deeper levels of a mutual human perception. It is a quality of being in touch with the reality of another individual.

It is a mutual openness of sharing the experiences of each other's inner self.

Causes for intimacy problems

Marriage is the most complex of relationships. However, it's more than worth the effort because the development of intimacy is the key ingredient to a fantastic marriage including meaningful sex. The vast majority of couples reach barriers that tend to take center-stage in their marriages.

The following are some of the potential intimacy robber which could destroy a healthy marital relationship. In the romantic interpersonal relationship, value system, individual perspective, level of education, backgrounds of family, faith, financial, social, and life goals determine a couple's compatibility. A relationship breaking up will most often be a result of incompatibility in different areas mentioned above.

We can bring past actions and attitudes that are wrong and damaging into the present, and find they sabotage our present experience and relationship with our spouse. Whether they are from yesterday or from the last decade, the past must be dealt with before we can go forward. This is the beauty of asking for forgiveness!

Conflicting values, standards, morals, ethics, and ideals with the other partner makes compatibility impossible. For example, if you and your partner have major differences in value systems, ethical issues, ideological issues or deep religious convictions, then compatibility reaches a deadlock. Coming to a meeting point for an agreement on values and beliefs will be an enormous step forward in eliminating intimacy problems.

As a barrier to intimacy, habitually viewing pornography sets up two formidable walls between couples - distressing guilt feeling and impractical sexual outlook. Husband, naturally feel guilty about a pornographic addiction, and usually try to hide it from their spouse. Of course, this dishonest behavior makes the genuine intimacy almost impossible. All the rationalizing, explaining, or defending of actions won't change the fact that a husband addicted to porn can't be intimate with his wife. A wife cannot win the competition with her husband's fantasies.

Let's face it, to change priorities is difficult. In actual fact, rearranging what we deem to be important rarely happens with most people. Over time, habits and lifestyles allow stress and fatigue, to crowd out intimacy and the spontaneous joys of marriage. As someone with a large family, many responsibilities, and no end of things to do, people find stress and fatigue to be a problem. Nothing kills intimacy faster than these intimacy robbers.

There is no hard and fast rule or quick fix for a new couple who has had previous romantic relationships that have gone astray or unhealthy. It mostly takes time, hard work, commitment, and effort for trust to grow and eventually blossom into physical, emotional and spiritual intimacy.

Some men see relationships as a machine which if it is not working, he quickly wants to replace the machine, and get the thing up and running again. A woman, on the other hand, tends to see a relationship as a plant that is growing, requiring nurture and attention. Intimacy grows just like a plant which grows steadily in the garden.

The influences of incorrect attitudinal thinking towards sex can damage intimacy. One can overcome intimacy problems by simply committing yourselves as a couple to doing whatever needs to be done to promote intimacy between you two. Intimacy involves a tenderness and tolerance as they are, letting another individual care for and acknowledge them as they are, always willing to respect each one's own uniqueness while it brings two people together in a dedicated relationship.

The Pillar of Commitment

The term 'commitment' means a permanent bond with someone or something. It is the means of transportation to help to grow deeper in love and safety. It is a way to protect the marriage relationship even during complicated periods. A relationship is like running a marathon. There are highs and lows, challenges and rewards, frustration and joy and sometimes the feeling of giving up and not continuing.

Commitment is defined as "awareness, an attitude, a clear and meaningful recognition of being fully present in the moment, making the choice of the moment, and standing by the consequences of these choices whether anticipated or not."[2] Commitment is a willingness to accept and live with both the strong and weak behavior of a spouse in the marital relationship. Commitment cannot be a single-minded decision; it has to be a mutual agreement to share together in the coming days. Through commitment, each is open to compromise and dialogue with the other.

A healthy relationship involves a day-to-day 'commitment' for the rest of their lives with dedication. Commitment has a twin role in a marital relationship. For a lifelong marriage, commitment is even more important than desirability and excitement. Underneath every commitment there should be devotion and dedication. Only under the soil of real, genuine commitment, can trust and deep intimacy grow.

The covenant relationship is based on a loving, compassionate, and truthful relationship. The exchange of vows during the time of the wedding ceremony is a sign of a relationship of continual love, care and faithfulness. The love is unconditional, a divine love (agape) that dwells within our heart for the one to whom we are living for. As we practice the unconditional love shown by our master Jesus Christ, we are able to love our spouse as he loves the church. Covenant partners manage unconditional love, forgiveness, and reconciliation while providing comfort and hope to their spouse. A covenant is built on selfless love, which means love is freely given and freely received. As strange as it may sound, a covenant marriage is one in which the 'tie that binds' the couple together is a dedication freely offered with no strings attached. Paul said it well 'Love never fails...' (1 Corinthians 13:8). This is the basis for mutual caring and faithfulness in all the marital relationships.

There are certain components of commitment in every marriage, namely spiritual, personal, and social commitment.

Take accountability and responsibility for the proceedings- As a spouse in a covenant marriage relationship, we are accountable for every action we make to remain in 'sexual purity' in all the relationships especially in our thoughts, actions and deeds towards our spouse.

Commitment is based on free will to choose. Commitment allows love and intimacy to mature over time. Someone who ends a relationship because the excitement of new love has diminished misses out on the opportunities that relationships bring for individual and mutual growth.

Most researchers, writers and theologians agree that commitment is the key to a successful marriage. Psychologist, counselor and author, Neil Clark Warren writes, "Marriage can be so difficult and requires so much toughness that, as a society, we ask persons entering marriage to take some hard-hitting, heavy duty vows. We know how easy it will be for them to give up along the way, to claim that they didn't know marriage would be so demanding. We gather into small or large groups just to hear them take these vows, and the people who are already married know that there are going to be times when these newlyweds will have to refer back to their vows – with the future of their marriage hanging in the balance."[3]

The commitment of marriage is not just for the wedding day or a certain period of time but is a continuous process. Scott Stanley, author of 'The Power of Commitment' reminds us, "Commitment is not about making a choice once and for all, on one day at the start of a marriage; it is about making many right choices every day and every week and every month. For example, there are many opportunities you will have in a life together where you can choose to give to your mate with the kind of love that propels a marriage beyond mere stability to dynamic vitality."[4]

Bill Doherty in his book 'Intentional Marriage' describes that in marriage, real commitment must lead to different kinds of achievement, which creates 'dynamic vitality.' According to Doherty the word 'intentional' means to be aware that your marriage requires high priority in developing a way of life, rituals and skills which cultivate commitment to constantly develop and sanitize the skills which support a happy and healthy marriage. Doherty believes that a committed or intentional couple "thinks about their relationship, plans for their relationship, and acts for their relationship, mostly in simple everyday ways and occasionally in big splashy ways."[5]

Marriage is a lifetime commitment of love, and trust. Husbands are commanded to love their wives as Christ loved the church. How did Christ love the church? He loved the church, which he calls his bride to the point of his death. Lifetime commitment means 'death do us part.' It is a challenging choice one has to make in his lifetime.

When we are committed to our spouse, we are to love each other unconditionally. Our love for our spouse is given in obedience to Christ, not in answer to our spouse's performances. If we love our spouse conditionally, we are in big trouble, because we never know when we are loved and when we are not.

Mutual commitment builds oneness in the life of partners which strengthens the marriage relationship as a unified attempt. This does not mean that spouses are the same or identical but they come from different entities. Oneness in marriage means being in agreement with God's will and purpose in the marital life. It is the mutual love of a man and woman sharing their lives together for a healthy marriage. They are for each other, and mutually complement each other; they are interdependent of each other. It can be explained in a diagrammatic way- vertically there should be oneness with God and horizontally with each other. One's personal relationship with God is very important and it will affect how you relate yourself with your spouse. The more the husband and wife are drawn closer to God, the greater the possibility for both experiencing oneness in marriage.

Marriage is a partnership with each other and a team effort by both spouses. Jesus committed himself to the Church and gave his life as an expression of his self- sacrificial love. Without the personal commitment to God, the trust will become dead and the norms of living will become empty and unproductive. Total commitment is like a personal relationship with God, with all the obligations, demands, challenges, fears and vulnerability that flow from this. With real personal commitment, the truths will become alive; the norms of living become spontaneous and natural, and respect becomes life-giving. Total commitment to each other may bring fear and a sense of vulnerability because we do not know what the relationship might ask of us. We can fear that we might be asked to enter more deeply into ourselves and to rise closer to becoming all that we are capable of being. These are profound thoughts and they can cause profound fears. Many people hold back from such a commitment and seek to be somehow in control of the relationship. They make sure they keep a certain distance from it. They can be polite and say all the right things, but without actually having to say and mean anything as committing and frightening as 'I love you irrespective of who you are forever.' And yet holding back and half-hearted commitments, inevitably harms the personal relationship, and the obligations become more burdensome and unproductive. Without a personal commitment to the other, truths will become lifeless, norms of relating will be a burdensome task and respect will be empty.

Endnotes

[1] Susan Heitler, *The Power of Two: Secrets to a strong and loving marriage* (Oakland, California: New Harbinger Publications, 2003) https:// www.amazon. in/Power-Two-Susan-Heitler/dp/1572240598

[2] William Horosz, *The Crisis of Responsibility: Man as the Source of Accountability* (Norma, Oklahoma: The university of Oklahoma Press, 1975), 248.

[3] Commitment: The essential ingredient in your marriage - *http://www. examiner.com*

[4] Scott M Stanley, *The power of commitment: A Guide to Active Lifelong Love* (San Francisco: Jossey-Bass, Inc, 2005).

[5] William J. Doherty, Ph.D., is a professor and director of the Marriage and Family Therapy Center at the University of Minnesota and co-founder of Family Life First. He has been named one of the ten most innovative therapists in the United States by Utne Reader. https://marriagemissions.com/living-an-intentional-marriage-marriage-message-165/ William Doherty, University of Minnesota, Intentional Marriage: Your Rituals Will Set You Free. *www.drbilldoherty.org*

10

Solving Conflicts in Marriage Relationships

The greatest marriages are built on teamwork.
A mutual respect, a healthy dose of admiration,
and a never- ending portion of love and grace

Fawn Weaver

E very marriage runs into blockades sometime or other. If both spouses learn how and when to recognize them and keep an eye on relationship problems before they occur, there is a better chance of thrashing them and keeping control of unhealthy relationships.

Discord, disharmony, friction, difference of opinion, belittling, ego clashes, constant and never-ending arguments, abusing each other physically, socially, emotionally, psychologically and spiritually are some of the factors which lead to bitterness in marital relationship. Every family member irrespective of caste, creed, religion or even denomination faces, disagreements, differences of opinion, and soft or harsh arguments. This is quite natural. These factors can lead to mental or physical illness, withdrawal symptoms from spiritual life, abuse of different sorts, and unhealthy relationships which lead to separation or divorce. Most unhealthy behaviours break out due to ego clash, lack of humility and concern for each other, and not knowing how to tackle the situation or how to discuss disagreements.

Many times, resentment is not because of something the spouse has said or the way they behaved or act, but through arguments or an unwillingness to compromise.

It is wise to ask why one's spouse is discouraged, frustrated, or disappointed. An attempt to avoid or ignore conflict altogether is not healthy. Conflict provides the possibility of growing closer and clarifying personal or family goals. Conflict is a distasteful and unpleasant fact that we all have some experience at some point of our life. Whether in the workplace, with friends, relatives, between husband and wife, parent and child; conflicts are sometimes unavoidable. Attempting to harmonize our relationships with others is a great task. It is always better to resolve a conflict when it arises before it gets worse. Once it takes a turn for the worse, the healing process may take time.

Conflict is also a part of our lives. As with any other partnership, couples will always face conflict because they both come from different backgrounds and value system. Despite the fact that the intensity of conflict varies in each relationship, it is also true that high frequency of conflict will adversely affect a relationship. There is a saying in the business world, conflict is good, too much conflict and less conflict is unhealthy and bad. There are numerous issues which are faced by the couples and a few are described below.

Decision Making

There are two ways we can approach the decision-making process in our life. Sometimes we have ample time to make a decision, other times we really do not have time at all. We have to make quick and fast decisions. Day by day make minor, major, long- or short-range decisions in our personal life with our spouse, children, parents, work area and so on. All these decisions can have a positive or negative effect and most of these decisions can have a future oriented effect. Therefore, we need to make decisions wisely and prayerfully. Joint decisions are always better, so that in the mere future there is no chance of finding fault with others. We need to make mature decisions that will make our family stronger. Wrong and hasty decisions can spoil marriages. Therefore, make good decisions at the right time.

Finance
In certain families we find spendthrift spouse, comparing finances with others and ending up in debt. Some have a tendency to put money in future savings rather than spending for the needs of the present. A wife may earn more than the husband creating conflicts, one spouse may give the financial support to the extended family without the knowledge of the spouse or take loans without any plans of paying back. There may be lack of sufficient income to spend due to poor mismanagement of money, fighting when there is less money in hand due to overspending, tension regarding payment of bills on time. Stress over money constitutes regular marital disharmony. This can happen due to different value systems, or priorities, incapability of handling money, or lavish spending or any other issues related to money. Nevertheless, during the crisis stage, financial stress could really lead to more anxiety and conflict.

It is advised that the couples should always be honest about their up-to-date financial situation with each other. Come to a consensus. If one has a tendency to spend more than the other, try to generate a budget and strive to follow it. Never hide debts. Never blame each other if debts occurs. Decide together who pays for what, so monthly dues are paid on time. Even if there are sufficient fund today, learn to save for the future.

The remedy for this problem is to prepare a financial budget for your family. Jointly decide the income and expenses. The budget should include food, education for the children, rent for accommodation, hospitalization, fuel, transportation, vacation, hospitality, repairs and maintenance, retirement, parental and sibling care, tithes, family and savings. Constant review is essential. The couple should open a joint bank account to manage these issues and deposit the major amount of their income. After that, you may open individual accounts if you think it is necessary. This is your personal money you can freely spend. In certain families the couples decide that one person will be managing the family finances. In some other family the house rent is paid by one, and other expenses are taken by other. Both husband and wife have separate bank accounts and they also manage the money separately.

Financial problems in a marriage are very common, irrespective of if one person is working, or both people are working, or no one is working. Money is always important, and agreeing on what to do with it can be difficult for even the most like-minded people. Money issues come when one person thinks they have more right to the money than the other person, can handle the money better than the other person, or is owed more than the other person. Handling finances effective, prudently and wisely is an art.

Children
According to Psalm 127:3, "Sons are a heritage from the Lord, children a reward from him." Children are the gift from God, however bringing them up in a Godly manner is challenging. Rearing children brings potential family problems if the priorities of husband and wife are different. Again, the Psalmist is cautioning us in verse 4, "Like arrows in the hands of a warrior......" We can mould them

whichever way we want to while they are young. Therefore, couples need to train them prayerfully and according to the word of God.

Working parents need to make many adjustments to take care of the children. The majority of women say that they feel less satisfied with their relationship with their husband after having babies, or growing children. Caring for children will reduce the amount of time the couples have together. Therefore, jointly nurture them, so that they can find time for each other. If it is a inter -religious, inter-caste or inter- race marriage more challenges are anticipated. Many times, the couples are blamed for not up bringing the children according to the family tradition or Biblical manner.

Wisdom, knowledge, strength and everything necessary for bringing up the children comes from God alone and not through any other media or friends. They should share the general responsibilities, of household chores and caring the children.

For married couples who expect to have children, the failure to have them can be shocking and upsetting. The 'blame game' starts. Family members compare them with sibling who have children. Showing partiality within the family can worsen the situation. It can be either the medical condition of the husband or wife. Finances for treatment, making adjustments in the work area, and following a strict treatment regime can be quite stressful. The future plans of a family can be crushed, and that can be hard on a couple who were looking forward to a future generation.

Mixed Priorities

The spouse who considers work, office, finance, parents, friends, electronics and social media more than husband or wife knowingly or unknowingly invites problems in the marriage.

All these are needed and necessary, however they must learn to give top priority for the family. Otherwise you should not be surprised if the relationship falls apart. Plan to go out together and be alone and treat it like any other major event on your calendar. Express appreciative words, greet each other with a happy face, give praise, show interest and respect to each other.

Infidelity

Extra marital affairs are in the limelight more than in the past. Couples continuing past affairs, making new friends of opposite sex in the work area, or getting acquainted through social media, cross the line of control and bring disharmony in the family. The children suffer more than the couple. There are many murders reported where the husband and his paramour killed the wife and children or vice versa in many parts of India.

Infidelity is a problem in some marriages. Affairs are usually used as a way to lick one's wound and to escape from the difficulties of the marriage. If your connection to your partner is lacking, begin by looking at what you are bringing to the party. If you are unfulfilled in the relationship, maybe it is because you are not offering all you could. You should be willing to do whatever it takes to re-establish the trust that was lost. The one and only remedy is to keep yourself pure and to be committed to God and to each other.

Inter-Faith, inter-Race and Inter-Caste Related Issues

In the beginning marriage seems to be alright. Later conflicts may arise due to faith related issues regarding customs and practice.

Sex

Sex is not everything in marriage, but it plays a great role in a healthy, stable marriage. Abstain from sex or disagreements in this area can worsen a marital crisis and is also a major sign of discord in marital relationships. Mary Jo Fay, author of "Please Dear, Not Tonight," says "Sex brings us closer, releases hormones that help our body physically and mentally, and keeps the chemistry of a healthy couple at healthy levels."[1] Also, it helps to have sex in different places other than the bedroom.

A great number of people are living in a sexless marriage and it is a major cause of conflict in marriage. It reduces connection, trust, and attraction, and it can lead to the death of a marriage if it is not handled wisely. If it prolongs in marriage, seek out a sex therapist to figure out what is going wrong and how you can rectify it. Also seek help from a physician to rule out medical condition.

Having a healthy sex life is important. Trust is the best foreplay. It is normal if intimacy does not happen as spontaneously as before. It is necessary to understand that times change, responsibilities grow and that as we create a family we have less availability or desire. Plan to have intimate conversation and touch every day; even try sleeping embraced. Learn what he likes and teach him what you like. And remember that there is no one perfect at sex.

Communication

Good communication between spouses requires hard work and determination. All human relationships are afflicted by varieties of communication problems. This becomes worst in the marital relationship when one is addicted to electronic media, mobile phone, spending more hours before television, excessive use of the internet, or computer, spending majority of time with friends, or coming late from the work area without any concrete reason.

Make sure the number one priority in your life whenever you are together or with the family, is put away any appliances or your engagements. Speak softly and discuss the issues very politely in open places, rather than behind closed doors. Learn from each other a few rules, such as not interrupting each other while talking, listening actively without defending yourself. Couples need to be sensitive and control the unwanted body language. Listen without rolling your eyes up and down, do not stare at each other while you're conversing. Create an atmosphere that you are listening each other very keenly.

Undesirable, harmful, damaging, or destructive communication should be avoided. The problem in poor communication is misunderstanding, which means not understanding the partner's point of view in a proper, positive and healthy manner.

When couples do not communicate, it is likely that other problems will escalate to an extent where it becomes impossible to pacify each other. Experts recommend that married couples set aside specific time to discuss problems if any and make some rules to avoid unnecessary arguments.

Lack of Love, Concern, Care, Respect, Understanding, Kindness
Trust is a key element in a loving relationship. If you do not fully trust your spouse, the problem needs to be talked about and resolved as soon as possible. Be consistent and loyal and keep up your word in everything you do. Some spouse has the tendency to hide things from each other. But never hide anything from your spouse and avoid telling lies. It is better to have a disagreement over the truth than to spend the rest of your life with a lie hanging over you.

Developing trust is always one of the most important challenges. Remember, it is easy to lose trust, but regaining trust is much tougher. Psychologists suggest that keeping promises and doing exactly what you promised will go a long way to help regain that trust. In short, every marriage will have its ups and downs. The longevity and happiness of your relationship will depend on how fast you both handle the problems as and how they occur. The trick is to resolve the small issue before it becomes a big one.

Along the way, you can lose respect for your spouse. Your wife or husband seemed to be great in the beginning, but after you've seen all their faults, annoying habits, mistakes, and continuous problems, you can easily lose respect for them and hold them in such low regard that you don't even view yourself on the same level as them anymore. You may start to despise them if you have so little respect for them, and, of course, that is a one of the causes of marriage problems that will likely result in divorce if you are not careful.

Respect often comes from what we value. If we feel someone is being less than they should be, we lose respect for them. If we feel as if someone is hurting themselves and can't gain strength to do better, we lose respect for them. If we don't think someone is living the 'right' way, we lose respect for them. But all of those things are based from our values and opinions, not theirs.

Comparison
Don't we notice spouses comparing themselves with others with regard to job, position, status in the society, wealth, house, physical beauty, influence, intelligence, talented children, and social life and so on and so forth? This will cause jealousy, frustration, blaming self and each other, criticising, cause depression and hostility. A few may look for ways to make money unlawfully some other may think of extra marital relationships and very few may decide to withdraw themselves from all activities.

Couples should understand that each one is unique. We are created in the image of God and have worth and value. Therefore, there is no need to compare ourselves with others.

Living with a spouse who is argumentative, abusive, discouraging, quick tempered, hostile, emotionally unstable, manipulative, disorganized, pessimistic, defensive, and critical is difficult.

Psychologists suggest that one way to deal with it is to understand that you cannot change the behaviour of others. However, you are in full control of your own behaviour. As a result, try to control yourself and maintain peace by showing patience. Impatience is also another factor which leads husband and wife's relationships to become strained.

It is important for these issues to be addressed without fighting, or even raising your voice. Regular fights lead to issues like unpleasantness, constant ill- fighting, and minor or major abuse which finally end up in divorce.

Put your ego in one side. Learn to forgive and seek for forgiveness. Improvement and strong healthy relationship depend on two mature minds.

Work stress can exacerbate marriage problems that already exist. Financial stress, pressures at home or work area could test patience as well as optimism, leaving couple with less to give to one another emotionally.

To handle daily stress, you should spend time on meditating or playing sports to take control of your mental and emotional health.

What are the Biblical Principles to Resolve Conflicts in Marriage?

In many marriages, couples do not want to sort or resolve issues in the marriage, face reality or spend time and effort trying to mend the relationship. This often means that the partners quit the marriage and they long for starting a fresh relationship with someone else.

God's word has the final authority to answer for every struggle we face in life. Proper guidance and counselling are needed to help couples with serious marital problems or those who are struggling to cope with their marital relationships. Couples need to believe that God is able to heal their broken relationships and mend the relationship much stronger than ever before. For this, one needs to have a strong unwavering faith in the Almighty God.

God created marriage. After all his creations on each day, he said it is good. However, God said that it is not good for man to be alone. He created woman, Eve for Adam. Therefore, God never intended hostility, bitterness and resentment between partners.

In 1 John chapter 5, verses 1-12 talks about faith in the Son of God. 1 John 5:4 says, "… for everyone born of God overcomes the world. This is the victory that has overcome the world, even our faith." The world here includes all evil and sinful patterns of life. There is victory over all these forces through faith in his word and in him. We need God's strength and power to overcome all evil forces.

The following are few principles to apply to repair and restore unhealthy or broken relationship in marriage.

The first and the foremost principle is *not to **GIVE UP** but have **FAITH** in the Almighty God.* Many couples have arguments quite often and have differences, which may lead to the loss of hope for the marriage. Some couples may resent each other so much that it may seem easier to give up on their marriage and avoid further complications. Therefore, they seek a way out by means of separation or divorce.

There are two options. Either you can give up or withstand with the issues. Why people are giving up? The simple answer is that there is no hope for an amicable solution from the issues they are facing.

This is the negative side of the issue. Why people are withstanding? There is a hope for the issues they are facing. They strongly believe that God is in control. This is a positive side. It is not easy to face marital problems and deal with the pain and wounds that have been inflicted. A child of God always looks at the positive side. No one can solve issues very easily or in a day. Sometimes it is a long process. It is hard work from the side of the couple, but with the power of the Holy Spirit, everything is possible.

The second principle is to **surrender *to God*.** The important step to improve the relationship is to surrender themselves and their marital relationship to the marvellous hand of the Almighty God. That is the best thing we can do as a human being. In order to do this, we need to have a mind of humility and have strong faith in the Almighty God.

The third principle is *to **pray for your spouse**.* Jesus said, "Pray without ceasing." In Matthew 6:6 " …when you pray, go into your room, close the door and pray to your Father who is unseen." Our God is a prayer answering God. There is a wise saying, "The couple who prays together stays together." The apostle Paul in 1 Thessalonians 5:16, "… pray continually." Through prayer one gets the adequate energy, motivation, and strength to overcome or withstand marital problems.

The biggest mistake people make during the marital discord is to break up and run away from the reality. God will hear our heartache and give a solution. There is a hope in the Lord. Continue to pray for guidance and strength from God to face challenges in marital life. When a family faces serious problems, how much time does one spend in prayer, individually or in togetherness, and trust in the power of the Almighty to answer all the challenges? When problems arises, some stop praying. Others pray alone rather than praying together. A few others request others to pray for them. When couples face difficulties there is only one option before them, to hand over the problems to God and seek guidance and strength to overcome the difficulties. For this, we need to look at Biblical authority - to respect, study and practice biblical principles rather than depend on human feelings, understanding, knowledge or wisdom of this world. Human feelings and wisdom cannot solve the challenges in marital life.

Philippians 4:6-7, "...but in everything, by prayer and petition, with thanksgiving, let your requests be known to God." The very next verse says peace of God. Peace of God in our life comes only through peace with God. Peace with God only prevails through absences of sin and possessing a forgiving spirit. We need to have an assurance that our sins are forgiven. 1 John 5:14, "...if we ask anything according to his will, he hears us."

The fourth principle is to connect *spiritual intimacy with your spouse.* Another important step to improve a troubled marriage is for the couple to pursue spiritual intimacy together. Spiritual intimacy and stability can be brought about by having regular morning and evening family prayer, reading and studying the word of God, going to church, taking part in church activities together.

The fifth principle is to *forgive and forget.* Often there are offenses on both spouses, but one need to be willing to forgive and forget for betterment and joyful living. There are few steps to be kept in mind, confession, godly sorrow, true repentance, and reconciliation. In 1 John 1:9, "If we confess our sins, he is faithful and just and will forgive us our sins and purify us from all unrighteousness." From this verse there is an assurance that if we confess from our human side, then God will forgive and restore us from all unrighteousness.

In the long run every spouse will hurt his or her partner in some way or other knowingly or unknowingly. It is important that couples must use the step of forgiving the spouse by Godly love. That is agape love. When we forgive there aren't any opportunities for bitterness, hatred, unloving and unconcerned behaviour.

The sixth principle is to *seek help when need arises.* Seeking help or support from mature and Godly counsellors as you work through marital problems is not a bad affair or sin at all.

King Solomon gives us a warning, "...but pity the man who falls and has no one to help him up!" (Ecclesiastes 4:10). This principle can be applied in our marital relationship also. Most of the marriages end up in bitter experience or divorce because couples have no one to support and encourage them as they work through problems. They want a moral support for restoration. The support of a Godly marriage counsellor, priest or a matured married couple whose life is exemplary can serve as their mentors, to repair the relationship.

Church need to play a great role in helping families to prevent conflicts. Many couples find it difficult to approach a marriage counsellor, but friends and family can persuade them to do so. Spiritual leaders with the right and apt words, knowledge, and insight can help both partners to understand each other, assist in recognizing and solving their conflict.

Endnote
[1] Mary Jo Fay, *Please Dear, Not Tonight: The Truth About Women And Sex: What They Want, What They're Not Getting* (London: Out of the Box Publisher, June 30,2006).

11

Marital Counselling

Marriage is over in an hour,
and yet it takes a lifetime to be really married

E. Stanley Jones

Three important things essential for a happy marriage are good memories of the past, forgiving and forgetting past mistakes, and a strong commitment to married life –the motto should be 'never give up whatever it may.' The apostle Paul in Philippians 3:13 says, "...forgetting what is behind and straining toward what is ahead."

In the earlier days, not much importance was given to pre-marital and continued counselling. That is no longer true. Things have changed, and Biblical principles are not emphasized in the life of many. In recent years much importance is given for pre-marital counselling. Along with Christians, there is an increasing number of non-religious couples seeking guidance too.

People tend to copy from their forefathers, relatives, friends and neighbors. Some of their false beliefs, traditions and customs have crept into the marital life leading to challenges and struggles in relationships. Men and women entering into a marriage covenant in the present age are no exception. Anxieties and challenges seem to be on the rise for married couples today. One couple arranged a prayer meeting as to celebrate their second wedding anniversary. The husband said he believes that if any couple completes two years of marriage successfully, there is no need to worry as they will have a long, happy, trouble-free marriage. This is not true as challenges will come later on also.

Many people are unprepared for marriage and confused about their roles and responsibilities. Many needs competent help from clergy, pastors, counselors and mature believers. Some are confused about the difference between morality and immorality. Sexual immorality has increasingly become normal among many Christians, even in our country. Pornography channels, and movies are easily accessible and available twenty-four hours a day. Many children, youths, adults and even senior citizen indulge in this. In the pretext of using the internet for educational purposes, children and youth watch pornography whereas their computer illiterate parents think that the children are using it for their studies. This has a bad effect as it can prompt them to have sexual relationships before marriage with single or multiple partners, explore perverted sex, or later have extra- marital relationships.

Most of the struggles in marriage originate not from outside, but from inside. A couple may prepare for marriage through premarital counselling, or from regular sermons from the pulpit on Christian marriage and family. This is needed so that those who enter into marriage are confident, may not be self-centered, and will accept the headship of Christ.

Premarital Counselling

According to John Henderson, "A healthy preparation for marriage requires you to grow in your understanding of what marriage is really about according to God's design and intention. Marriage originates with God who determined it, created it, and assembled its essential parts. God formed marriage between a husband and wife to display his glory, especially the glory of Christ and the church. Marriage offers a visible, living picture of God's redeeming love. In a related way, marriage provides a means to expand the kingdom of Christ by producing children and training them to love God and further his kingdom purposes. Through marriage, God grants to you a suitable companion for your life on earth, someone to help you become less self-absorbed and more oriented to another, someone for God to use in conforming you to the image of Jesus Christ."[1]

I have a friend whose son was getting married.[2] On the previous day of marriage the parish priest met both the bride and bridegroom for the first time. It was in the pretext of premarital counselling. He asked the bride 'do you know how much your would-be- husband is earning?' She said 'no.' The priest continued, 'you both talk, I will pray and leave now as I'm little busy.' I still wonder what the couples would have gained through this so called 'premarital counselling.'

Premarital counselling is defined as a counselling offered by a marriage counselor, or a clergy, to help a couple to prepare for marriage and their day to day life in a Godly manner. According to J. Kenneth Morris, premarital counselling is "a form of counselling which centers around the interpersonal relationship of a man and a woman, helps them evaluate their relationship in view of their approaching marriage and acquaints them with ways by which they may build happy and successful marriage, or in the light of the evaluation of their relationship, results in their deciding against the marriage."[3]

In his definition, Morris speaks on interpersonal relationship and evaluation of that relationship. Another definition says that, "it is a type of therapy that helps couples prepare for marriage."[4] In other words, it is a form of counselling that can benefit any individual who is planning to get married. It has an educational factor in it and will help couples to learn the skills they will need to support them in a happy, healthy and a lasting marital relationship. It also will help a couple to identify and communicate about their fears, anxiety, desires, beliefs, values, dreams, needs, and other issues that were previously avoided or denied, and never discussed before. Premarital counselling is necessary to strengthen the marriage before it takes place by preparing for and anticipating challenges and conflicts that could arise in the marriage in the future. As a result of successful premarital counseling, the counselees get to know each other better.

In the premarital counselling session, the counsellor is likely to bring up topics that they have never thought or discussed earlier. Even if the couple think that they know each other well, they might still be surprised, to learn new things about each other. Counsellor assist them in getting to know each other through transparency in conversation, revealing future plans, and expectation, learning how to support each other's dreams and how to dismantle their own fears. Counselling increase communication and problem-solving skills and teaches one to listen.

Improving Communication Skills

It is important to fully understand the way you and your partner receive, send, process, and share information. Premarital counselling may be a good time to exercise your listening skills. Each individual handle the conflict, problems, and emotional issues differently. The communication and conflict-resolution skills that one gains during premarital counselling can help in the marital relationship. When couples go for counselling, they talk individually or collectively to the clergy. Inevitably they can build better communication skills because they have a neutral party, a qualified and experienced person, to help or guide them in understanding one another. No doubt this is one of the biggest benefits of premarital counselling. In addition to learning how to better communicate, individual needs and desires, couples also learn how to better understand each other. The clergy's main goal in counselling is to attain in the life of couple self-actualization, self-realization, self-dependent, self-satisfaction, self-understanding, self-exploration and maturity.

Gaining Insight in Many Areas

Counselee may gain insight in areas like intimacy, affection, sex, finance management, crisis management, expectations, beliefs and values, children and parenting, decision making, conflict resolution, dealing with anger and emotions, and role models in marriage. Discussing these topics help the couple to solve them before it takes them by surprise. Expectations within the marriage can fall into different areas which may differ from individual to individual. Discussing expectations with real understanding and respect leads to working together and solving challenges effectively. This can help to remove resentment and hurt.

Helping with Financial Management

One of the main reasons why marriages turn bitter are because of financial issues. Many young people do not know what it takes to manage finances individually or collectively. Counselling explores the meaning of money to each partner and also teaches the couple financial skills even before they face the issues in real life.

Preparing themselves for Conflict Management

Generally, two people never have identical values and goals in life. It is important to identify any possible conflicts before they even occur. Conflicts are some of the most difficult things couples face in the marriage. Because conflicts can increase problems in relationships, it is important to develop strategies to limit and reverse these. Counselling helps to identify potential conflicts if any and teach them ways of resolving these.

Identify a Common Vision for the Family

To have a successful marriage, the couples need to have a shared vision. The vision is a conscious and careful means of creating the relationship together towards the destination 'until death'. It also helps them assess whether they are together in their relationship.

Understand Compatibility

Premarital counselling helps them determine if this is really the right time to tie the knot or wait for some more time, rather than making a hasty decision, and ruining a healthy marriage. It empowers the relationship and shows light in the dark or grey areas of life.

Objectives of Premarital Counselling

The following are the objectives of Premarital Counselling.

- To build a good and a healthy attitude towards a biblically based marriage.

- To provide an awareness about the solemnity of Christian marriage and teach what to do to avoid sin and how to handle sin in a Biblical manner when it comes.

- To explain Christian values and principles to adopt in marriage.

- To guide and nurture the couple and to train them and discipline when necessary.

- To teach what genuine love is and how to keep it going.

- To discuss the need for an open communication skill.

- To enlighten the couple about the areas of adjustment with each other for a better marriage.

- To highlight the importance of decision-making, making right decision at right time and learning problem- solving skills.

- To explain Christ model of marriage and how to say 'no' to temptation.

- To discuss human sexuality, sexual relationships, pregnancy and child rearing.

- To discuss time management, work- life balance, and leisure time.

- To give insight into financial management in family life.

- To give guidance on crisis management and conflict resolution.

- To discuss the law of the country regarding marriage registration, abortion, adoption, and spousal abuse.

The main objective of premarital counseling is not to solve the engaged couple's problems and make them perfect. No one can solve anybody's problems in a short period of time; only equip them with the valuable tools to solve their own problems in the days to come. As is often said, "Give a man a fish; you feed him for a day. Teach a man to fish; and you feed him for a lifetime." This is the principle of premarital counselling. No one can solve the entire problems one is facing in their life in an instant. This is a training period.

Counselors must understand that marriage is a brand-new entry for a lifelong relationship. The partners are of different backgrounds. Their family background, educational status, financial status, religious background, language, job, customs and habits may differ. There may be areas which might disqualify the couple for marriage after open discussion. They may have apprehensions about life-long commitment, uncertainties and anxiety as they enter into this new venture. They may have fears due to bitter experiences in their family, friends, films they watched or stories they read. Many lack knowledges of sexuality and sexual relationships, pregnancy, or may have false ideas of these. The counselling process should be flexible, and it need to be modified accordingly.

The counsellor must consider it as a valuable pastoral ministry. Through premarital counselling we are merging two individuals of different value systems and family backgrounds. If any couple wants to marry a non-believer, then first of all, the non-believer must come to the full knowledge of Christ. He or she must accept Jesus as their personal saviour. Many clergy will not consider pre-marital counselling if the engaged couples are not born-again Christians. Marriage is tough enough without being unequally yoked.

Premarital counselling normally falls under the spiritual responsibility of the pastoral care team. In recent years the clergy will not undertake to perform a marriage ceremony unless the engaged couple attends to a series of counselling sessions. The period of the premarital counselling varies from denomination to denomination. Pastors are aware of the blessings and challenges of marriage and want to help those they join in marriage to have successful ones. Premarital counselling plays an important part of helping couples enter into marriage covenant equipped and to build a strong union.

Some churches do not allow marriages to take place without regular pre-marital counselling and insist on a certificate stating that both the bride and bridegroom have attended pre-marital counselling before banns are published. There are a few churches which allow the couples to pay an enormous amount so that they are waived off from attending pre-marital counselling. A few churches permit the couples to attend premarital counselling within a year of marriage or pay an amount as penalty. In the above cases the benefit of the premarital counselling is nil. Rules for attending pre-marital counselling vary from church to church, financial status or influence of parents or couples, or whether residing in India or abroad.

Approach to Premarital Counselling

Premarital counselling sessions should address the following areas in order to assist the couples which include compatibility, personality, families of origin, communication, conflict resolution, intimacy and sexuality, and long-term goals. It is the time for an appraisal to find and evaluate their spiritual, physical and emotional maturity. This will give an idea whether they are ready for marriage or matured enough for a stable and God-honoring marriage. Not only emotional maturity, but one can also understand the compatibility or non -compatibility of the two personalities who can or cannot live together. It also opens a way to discuss their interpersonal relationship and need for open communication. The value system of individuals differs; hence open discussions will help them to learn about it together. The counselling session is an opportunity to test how far they are able to adjust emotionally and be sensitive and forgiving to each other. Respect and loyalty towards each other can be evaluated.

It is always good to ask questions and find answers before one enters the marital relationship. For many questions there should be an open discussion between the partners to find a solution. A counselor can assist them in answering these and clarify doubts.

A sample approach to pre-marital counselling is given in the following pages. Counselors should feel free to adapt according to their own gifts and style if all the essentials are covered, and it is based on Biblical principles. Each couple will have different levels of physical, mental, social and spiritual maturity. For some, if the marriage was arranged by their parents, there are meeting for the first time. Others have been dating for some time, a few have been married before, marrying again due to the death of the spouse or divorce. Children may or may not there. A few belonging to a different religious background, caste or creed. A few had been living together without wedlock but now want to get married. The scenarios differ. The counselling sessions should start and end with prayer. It is good to work with them based on scriptural passages. Basic principles of counselling should be followed. The questions given below will guide the Marriage Counselor in assisting the counselee to enter into a better, healthy and meaningful marital relationship.

Sample Questions to be asked During Premarital Counselling

Concepts of marriage
Why did you decide to get married?

Do you think premarital counselling will be helpful to you?

How did you both meet?

How long have you known each other?

How well you know each other?

Were you formerly engaged?

Do you have parental consent?

What are the factors that influenced you to select your partner for a lifelong relationship 'until death'?

Why do you want to marry this person?

How do you propose to make the marriage successful, meaningful, so that it will not end up broken, unhealthy or in divorce?

What is your view about the role of the husband/ wife in marriage?

What are your views on a woman working after marriage or after the birth of the child?

Do you look forward to marriage with high expectation?

What is your idea of a romantic evening?

What may be considered to be the biggest battleground in marital life?

What is your attitude towards your future in-laws?

How do you view the rest of your spouse's family?

Do you think children need to be disciplined from a very young age?

How will you manage to discipline your children? Who will discipline?

To what extend will the qualities of love exist in your life?

Are you comfortable with your mate if he/she spends time with a person of the opposite sex?

Previous marriage

Why do you want to marry for the second time?

Did you disclose the reasons for second marriage?

If you are divorced, how much maintenance commitment do you have every month?

Do you have a child / children from the previous marriage?

Who is looking after the child / children?

Do you feel that you should have child / children along with children of your previous marriage? When? How many?

Mutual Expectations

Have you planned about the type of house to live in after marriage, thought about the kind of neighborhood and friendship you look forward to?

How do you intend to shape your children's value system?

Family

Can you describe your family of origin-socially/ economically/ spiritually/ financially/ and emotionally?

Are your parent's role models in private and public life? Do they lead a successful family life?

What are the good qualities you've observed in your parent's family life that you want to adapt to your family life?

Have you observed any drawbacks or failures in your parent's marriage which you do not want to repeat in your marriage?

What fine examples did your parents set in their marriage that you would like to follow?

Did your parents come from a broken family? Did this influence, affect you in any way?

Did you have a chance to interact with your would-be parents-in-laws? Are they practicing Christians?

How do you plan to find time to spend with your parents and siblings after marriage?

Do you expect your parents to stay with you after marriage?

Spiritual life

Are you and your spouse Christians? Have you both submitted your lives to Jesus?

How important is Jesus in your life? Are you confident that you are a born-again Christian?

Do you come from a home where there is a regular family prayer without any compromise? How much time do you both spent in individual and family prayer?

Do you regularly attend church and participate in church activities?

Do you have a commitment that on Sunday one needs to worship rather than engage in other activities?

Do you participate in Bible study groups, fellowship groups or other church-based interactive groups?

How does your spiritual life impact your life and inter-personal relationships?

Do you think that a married couple should have personal quiet time, personal and family devotion regularly along with your busy work schedule?

Do you think that your wife/husband is a gift from God, an answer to your prayers?

Have you shared your faith with your spouse?

Will you try to impose your personal convictions on your mate?

What are the uniting factors which make a perfect marriage?

What is the most important principle which builds a happy marriage?

Physical health
What are your hygiene habits?

What are your hobbies?

Do you take exercise regularly?

What health problems or major illness are there in your family?

What health problems do you have?

What is your belief about substance abuse?

What are your food habits?

Psychological health

Do you feel accepted and emotionally safe with your partner?

Do you feel loved and secure in your relationships?

How do you react when you are stressed? How do you handle stressful situations?

How do you behave when you are sad, depressed or angry?

Is it easy for you to accept a mistake?

Is it easy for you to forget and forgive a mistake made by your spouse?

How do you handle disputes and disagreements?

Are you treated like a child, though you are an adult? If yes, are you comfortable being treated in this manner?

In which area are you still emotionally immature?

Are you transparent with one another?

Sexual life

Do you believe that heterosexual marriage is the God intended culmination of sexuality?

Do you believe that heterosexual relationship is the most intimate human relationship?

Do you believe that meeting the sexual needs of the spouse can also determine the strength of a marriage?

Are you comfortable in talking about sexuality with your partner?

How important is sex in married life?

Do you believe sex is a gift from God to humankind?

Have you ever been sexually abused, assaulted or attacked by anyone? If so, how does this affect you - physically, mentally, spiritually and emotionally?

Do you know if the person you are going marry has been sexually abused, assaulted or attacked? How do feel about it and how do react to it? How well do you accept the person?

Did you have sex with anyone else? If yes, how do you feel about that right now?

In case the future spouse has already had sexual relations with someone else how do you react to it?

Are you looking forward to sexual intimacy? Scared? Indifferent?

Have you been addicted to pornography in the past?

What are your beliefs about sexual activities/ practices?

Social health
What are your favorite means of relaxation?

How do you spend your holidays…with family, friends, others?

What are your social responsibilities and commitments?

Financial management
Are you comfortable in pooling all the income and operating finances for the family from a single bank account?

What are your ideas about earning, saving, and spending your money?

What is your attitude about savings?   What are your viewpoints about spending? Who will make key financial decisions?

How important is money in your personal and marital life?

What are your priorities regarding finance?

What debts are you presently paying off?

Do you have a house of your own?

How do you view your career prospects?

What is your belief about tithing?

Are you expected to support your family financially? If so, for how long and how often?

If you intend to have different accounts, who will be responsible for expenses in the family?

Do you prepare a monthly budget, follow and review it often?

Budget
The following are areas of expenditure which may help the counselees to prepare a budget, especially for those who have not thought about it:

Income: Salary of both, income from other sources.

Expenditure:
Food: Provisions, eating out, guests,

Shelter: Monthly rent or yearly lease- housing, insurance, house maintenance. Gas, water and electricity bills, telephone or mobile bills.

Clothing: for family and relatives, for festivals and functions

Personal: visit to beauty salons, Spa, toiletries,

Tax payment:

Health: Regular checkup, sickness of family members, sudden illness, hospitalization.

Savings: joint savings, individual savings, fixed deposit,

Insurance: medical, life, vehicle, house

Family entertainment: Vacation trips, socializing,

Travel: four wheeler and two wheeler payments, gasoline, maintenance and repairs, hiring vehicles

Financial support: Parents, siblings, any other family members, organizations.

Children's education: School / College fees, extra tuitions, further studies

Personal Growth: Continuing education, purchasing books, subscribing for electronic media, newspaper, magazine.

Church Contribution: Tithes, church activities.

Donation: Institutions, relief funds, festivals, poor and needy.

Debts: Repayment of the loans, if divorced maintenance commitments.

Continued Counselling (Post - Marital Counselling)
Pre-marital counselling is a preparation session for one enter into real arena of marriage. But in the case of post-marital counselling, it is a practical session. We are practicing what we learn through theory

in the pre-marital class. Pre-marital counselling is mere rehearsal but facing realities of marriage can be challenging. Through post-marital counselling the church can save many marriages shedding light to the dark or grey areas of their lives. A church is considered to be vibrant when there are godly families. Therefore, the church must take a keen interest in post- martial counselling.

Challenges
A few major challenges faced by the couple as they start life together are highlighted here. It differs from family to family.

Communication Problems
Poor or lack of proper communication can lead to communication difficulties. Poor communication can crop up due to lack of clarity, no communication or because of confused thinking. Communication with one another is essential in keeping love alive.

Sex Life
There are many reasons why couples lose interest in sexual intimacy with their partner or struggle in showing physical affection. It may be due to unsatisfying sex, dissatisfaction in their sex life or and lack of frequency of sex. Declining frequency of sexual intimacy may be due to irregular work pattern, shifting duty time, being away from home for work, physical and mental tiredness due to heavy workload, less time together, unnecessary arguments, different bed timings and sleep pattern, or hygiene habits. It is important for spouses to find ways to keep their sex life live, fresh, and fulfilling. Women are more likely to experience lack of emotional intimacy than men. Dissatisfaction with her marriage, a loss of trust in her husband, and other relationship concerns can all affect emotional intimacy between two partners. When these concerns are not communicated, they can make a woman feel distant from her partner, and this can,

in turn, decrease her desire to be sexually intimate with him. If your sex life feels less than satisfying, don't expect it to get better on its own. Both have to make an effort to change it.

Considerable spiritual guidance should be given to married couples concerning the true nature of love as opposed to lust and indulgence. Too frequently marriage is considered to be a license for lust, and within the framework of the marriage relationship many, particularly men, seek to gratify their carnal natures by the most abominable forms of deviant sexual behavior. Such behavior brings a degrading influence into the home and a relationship that all too frequently develops an attitude of repugnance on the part of the wife. The sacredness of the marriage is lost to the satiation of sensual desires. Husbands and wives need much counsel concerning the literature they read and the films they witness, for no one can consistently read literature bordering on the pornographic or view suggestive pictures or films without their eroding the spiritual life that is so necessary to live a life according to God's will.

In this day of unrestricted contraceptive devices and abortions many Christians have lost their sensitivity to the true principles of Christian temperance in their interpersonal relationships in the home. The clergy needs to be very much aware of the development of guilt feelings so often associated with unrestrained sexual practice and with abortions—a guilt that cannot be overlooked or eradicated by simple platitudes- for deep within the consciousness of every Christian is the over-riding challenge of the purity of God.

Financial Problems
Financial problems include debt, hiding debts, an attitude of mine-yours-ours, hiding money, overspending, under spending, different ways of spending, financial abuse, lack of transparency in handling money, fighting for money on different occasions. Couples who

decide to keep their finances separate face issues when it comes to money. Discussing finances with your spouse can be stressful and tense, especially if the couple has different spending habits or ways of managing money. In order to avoid this issue, be sure that you and your spouse make a financial plan together and skip any unnecessary disagreements by staying focused on the situation at hand. Learning how to balance your spending habits and your financial situation is a tough hurdle that every newly wed couple will have to face.

Invading Spouse's Boundary

Spouse may sometimes try to make drastic changes in the life of his or her partner. It may be done intentionally, showing disrespect, anger, physical or emotional hurting, uttering unruly words, or personal invasion of the spouse's boundaries. Manipulative, dictative, or controlling actions of the wife by her husband by not allowing her to socialize and checking all her activities suspiciously may harm the marital relationship.

Fluctuating Priorities

When either spouse redirects their attention from the relationship to other interests - be it career, children, friends, spiritual or social activities, travel, spending more time on social media, electronic gadgets or hobbies, etc.- it can cause conflicts. Continue participating in your regular hobbies and activities. If one of you feels left out, invite each other to join or encourage him to take on a new hobby of his own. It's tough to manage busy schedules as married couple, especially when you also want to set some time aside for just yourself.

Children

Children are the 'bundle of joy' for every family. Families welcome a baby with great expectations. However, parenting affects not only children but also parents themselves. It will generate stress, sadness, frustration or depression. But as a mother's bond with a child grows, it's likely that her other relationships deteriorate. The relationship between spouses suffers once children come along. Some find it difficult, therefore they are forced to make adjustments.

In the event that a pregnancy is unplanned, the parents experience even greater negative impacts on their relationship.

The irony is that even as the marital satisfaction of new parents declines and having children may makes you miserable, you'll be miserable together. The biggest change after having children is the loss of freedom and autonomy.

Parents having a differently abled child is a lifelong adjustment they must make. Caring for such a child, accepting and tolerating their disabilities, loving them unconditionally need extra patience, good health and above all god's grace in abundance. The siblings are also affected. It is noticed in India that having only girl children may be distressing for the parents.

Work Life Balance

After leading an independent life before marriage, the couples find it difficult to balance work and family. In order to maintain a balance both of them must be willing to learn and adjust. Work pressure at office and home can ignite to become a major problem. They must keep communications open so that problems will not arise.

Faith Related

In any marriage breakup there has been a prior breakdown in spiritual life - family prayer, religious life within the home, regular church worship, fellowship meetings. Sometimes one partner will seek to one church and other may go to other church. It is essential to Christian marriage that the family altar be established in which a loving, spiritual relationship exists. Many fake priests' advice people to indulge in occult activities, practicing black magic, calling the spirits of the dead and visiting various temples to make easy money. If one of the spouses is a non-believer, their home will be distorted.

Health

Many times, health issues are not disclosed when marriages are fixed, especially psychiatric problems, long term illness, cardiac, renal diseases, congenital problems, gynecological issues, deafness, so on so forth. At times knowing the health condition of the spouse, the other one decides to marry mostly out of sympathy. In real situations, after marriage, it causes many problems, mistrust, misunderstanding, hostility, depression, etc. A sudden accident can cripple the family. Financial stress comes from long term treatment. Coping with all these factors will become difficult.

Facing Guilt

The role of the clergy, counsellors and matured Christians is to help the fallen and the people whose lives are threatened. There is no other area of life where feelings of guilt, shame, and remorse express themselves more frequently than in unclean and sinful behavior in marriage. Almost every congregation includes those who are suffering from the penetrating cancerous disease of practices that have violated the true and noble concept of marriage. Such men and women need to be brought to the full realization of a loving and forgiving God. God has declared, "Therefore, there is now no condemnation for those who are in Christ Jesus" (Rom. 8:1). For any marriage to succeed after a violation of its sanctity takes not only the forgiveness of God but also the forgiveness of the wronged partner. Many marriages could be rescued if the true principles of forgiveness were understood by both the sinned and the sinned against. Great wisdom and prayerful understanding are needed to fulfil each one's role effectively.

Selfishness and Mistrust

When appreciation between married couple is diminishing, conflict tends to rise. Every man and woman longs for positive recognition one way or other.

In some marriages, selfishness leads to controlling, manipulative, jealous, possessive and abusive behaviour. In order to prevent issues of selfishness in marriage, spouses must learn how to act with empathy and create a balance between both their own and their spouse's needs-physical, emotional, spiritual, and social. If one spouse acts selfishly and consistently places their own needs and desires ahead of their spouse's, then it will create unpleasant situations.

Without trusting each other it is impossible to have a healthy marriage. When a spouse cheats, tells lies, hides something, or breaks a promise, it can upset and wound the relationship. If the issues are not dealt within a specified time, the betrayed spouse will continue to feel hurt, pain, anger, and be suspicious about everything.

Forgiveness and trust are two different things which need to be recognized in marital life. If your spouse has broken your trust or you have broken theirs, forgiveness should be given instantaneously because grace can't be earned. However, trust has to be earned and it can only be earned slowly through consistency of action and hard work.

While it's normal for married couples to get angry with each other from time to time, it is important that both spouses act properly when situations arise. It's also vital that couples actively listen to each other, openly express their views or opinions, and avoid defensive behaviours.

Marriage counselling can help couples who simply want to strengthen their bonds and gain better understanding of each other. There is great scope for marriage counselling if domestic violence or abuse occurs in their marital life.

Unfaithfulness

Sexual dissatisfaction can be caused by lack of regular sexual contact, unfulfilling sex, unsatisfactory sex, sex frustration, a sexless marriage, aging, illness, or lack of sexual attractiveness. Sometimes couples expect the same excitement and fun they initially experienced with their partners. This is unrealistic in later years. The roots of all unfaithfulness are loneliness, neglect, unappreciated, emotionally irrelevant, fear of growing older, sadness, anger, resentment, boredom, disconnection from their spouse and feeling trapped, isolated, disrespected, insecure and bitter. A few examples of underlying issues that can cause infidelity include addictions, narcissism, intimacy disorders, and bipolar disorders.

In each of these instances, you can see that spouses cheat because their needs or their spouse's needs aren't being met in some way. Unmet needs are extremely hazardous to marriages – even happy ones.

Emotional Infidelity

It is not unusual for husband and wife to become emotionally disconnected to one another. This is where emotional infidelity has the opportunity to slip into the marriage. Emotional infidelity can be worse than physical cheating.

When your marriage is in crisis, everyone is going to have opinions about what you should do or not do. Listen to a God-fearing person, clergy you respect. Love your spouse and love God. Be careful and sensitive where you are getting advice.

When our car is broken, we don't have a problem taking it to a mechanic and when our arm is broken, we don't have a problem going to a surgeon, but for some reason, when our marriage is facing certain issues or broken, we think we need to figure it out on our own. Seek a Godly guidance or help from a clergy, mature Christians, or Christian counsellor. There are more resources in our churches today than in earlier days, so take full advantages of them.

The road ahead won't be easy or smooth, but your marriage is worth fighting for. Take it one day at a time, lean on each other, and trust God to take care of the rest 'until death'. Therefore '**never give up**.'

Endnotes

[1] John Henderson, *Catching Foxes- A Gospel -Guided Journey to marriage* (Phillipsburg, New Jersey: Presbyterian &Reformed Publishing Company, 2018).

[2] Personal interview in Chennai.

[3] J. Kenneth Morris, *Premarital Counselling: A Manual for Ministers.* (Prentice -Hall, 1965), 15.

[4] *www.mayoclinic.org prc-20013242.*

Conclusion

Women were created from the rib of man to be beside him,
not from his head to top him, nor from his feet to be trampled
by him, but from under his arm to be protected by him,
near to his heart to be loved by him

Matthew Henry

There was full media coverage on Valentine's Day 2019 and the news was about an event organised by NGO named 'Youth Nation' and 'Haseyamev Jayete'. Over 10,000 students of 20 schools and colleges in Surat, North India remembered Saint Valentine, the patron saint of love, the day dedicated to his memory, by taking a pledge not to marry without their parents' consent. The oath taking ceremony was held on school and college grounds in the presence of members of 'Youth Nation' and 'Haseyamev Jayete', local non-government organizations. Vikas Doshi, a volunteer of Youth Nation, said, "We are amazed at the response of the students. Parents play a very important role in their lives and hence they believe marriage should only happen with the consent of parents." Kamlesh Masalawala, laughter guru, one of those who organized the event said, "We have received positive response from across the city. People want our country's culture and traditions to be kept intact. Love can happen to anyone, but for that you can't reject your beloved parents. Youths have assured us that we are on right track as a society and nation."[1]

Traditionally girls are groomed in their respective families to become better wives in their marital life. Indian society spent much time in grooming the girls - developing various skills in cooking, sewing, cleaning, washing- disciplining them, making them to take care of children and elderly ones. Further they are taught to respect and obey all elders and men folks. They are also told to be silent when any abuse or atrocities happen. From very young age they are reminded that her home is temporary whereas after marriage she will be shifted to her husband's home which will be her permanent home in this earth. However this kind of grooming rarely happens in most of the boy's home. Boys are made to believe that women are subordinate as men are the bread winners and decision makers. Some boys are growing at home without a sister as a sibling. Therefore they may not understand the psychological, physiological or social needs of females.

The trends are changing now. Children realize and recognize the value of their parents and elders and that they should not take major decisions on their own. "Train a child in the way he should go, and when he is old he will not turn from it" (Proverbs 22:6). Never wait for teenage years. The parents must set good examples in front of their children to follow when they get married. Training and moulding character of children to be started at very young age by parents at home first. When parents lead as exemplarily family life, their children will learn to value marriage as a God ordained institution.

Marriage is instituted by God. This unequivocally means that people need to enter it on God's framework. It is to be a solemn, public, contractual relationship entered into voluntarily by an eligible Christian man and woman, for companionship, happiness, procreation, legitimate sexual relations, and the resulting transmission of gospel truths to children. As such, it is God who established and ordained marriage and the family. It is therefore the foundation of all social bonds and human activity.

God's plan for the marriage covenant involves the following vital principles:

The marriage is for permanence

Marriage is intended to be permanent, since it is established by God (Matthew 19:6; Mark 10:9). Marriage represents a sober and prayerful commitment that no one should enter into it lightly or ill advisedly. It involves a solemn promise or pledge before God.

Divorce is not permitted except in very limited Biblically prescribed circumstances. In the Old Testament, in the books written by Moses, divorce is permitted and regulated (Deuteronomy 24:1-4; Leviticus 21:7, 14; 22:13, Numbers 30:9) in ancient Israel. Whereas in New Testament Jesus said "……..anyone who divorces his wife, except for marital unfaithfulness, causes her to become an adulteress, and anyone who marries the divorced women commits adultery" (Mathew 5:32). Even in such cases, divorce is only permissible, but not encouraged or even preferred. Jesus insisted that marriage according to God's original design was lifelong and permanent, based on the statement in Genesis that a man will leave his father and mother and hold fast to his wife, 'and the two will become one flesh' (Matthew 19:5, citing Genesis 2:24). Jesus insisted on this principle and concluded that, "Therefore what God has joined together, let man not separate" (Matthew 19:6).

There must be a commitment and determination to cleave together in good and bad times. Divorce is not the solution to every physical, spiritual, financial or emotional problem in the marital life. God never intended divorce for couples who are entering into a marital relationship. God expects a stable and God honouring marriage.

Marriage is Sacred

Marriage is not merely a human agreement between two consenting individuals for a 'civil union'. It is more than that. It is a relationship before and under God's authority (Genesis 2:22). Therefore God condemn same-sex marriage, homosexual and lesbian relationships. God will never sanction a marital bond between two members of the same sex.

Marriage is for Intimacy

Marriage is the most intimate of all human relationships, uniting a man and a woman in a 'one-flesh' union (Genesis 2:23-25). Marriage involves 'leaving' one's family of origin and 'being united' to one's spouse, which signifies the establishment of a new family unit distinct from the two original families of the husband and wife. While 'one flesh' suggests sexual relationship and normally procreation, at its very heart the concept entails the establishment of a new relationship between two previously unrelated individuals (and families) by the most intimate of human bonds before God.

Marriage is for Mutuality

Marriage is a relationship of free self-giving of one human being to another (Ephesians 5:25-30). The marriage partners are to be first and foremost concerned about the well-being of the other person and to be committed to each other in steadfast love and devotion. This involves the need for forgiveness and restoration of the relationship. Scripture is clear that wives are to submit to their husbands and to serve as their 'suitable helpers,' while husbands are to bear the ultimate responsibility for the marriage before God (Ephesians 5:22-24; Colossians 3:18; Genesis 2:18, 20).

Marriage is an Exclusive Relationship

Marriage is permanent, sacred and intimate, (Genesis 2:22-25; 1 Corinthians 7:2-5), further there should not be any other human relationship to interfere with the marriage commitment between husband and wife. For this reason, Jesus treated sexual immorality of a married person, including even a husband's lustful thoughts, with utmost seriousness (Matthew 5:28; 19:9). Premarital sex is also illegitimate, since it violates the exclusive claims of one's future spouse.

The dreams, potential and expectations of any individual entering into the matrimonial relationship are ample. For many, marriage and family life means having a positive and permanent healthy relationship. Marriage and family life are the original idea of God with an intention for better relationships to avoid loneliness in an individual's life. Family, Church and Community are three indivisible institutions according to Genesis 2:23. In traditional Christian Marriage, the vows of commitment are an important factor, "…for better or for worse, for richer or for poorer, in sickness and in health, till death us do part."[2] Even though marriages are made up of two sinful and imperfect people who resist under the yoke of sin, when they commit themselves to the hands of God, he will make imperfect people perfect.

In the book of Genesis, we will be able to see that there were family breakdown and failures in their family system due to rivalries, conflict, lying, deception, spousal abuse, childless couples, sexual abuses, strained relationships between parents and children. Satan always has a close eye on strong and healthy families to weaken their family life. Therefore, we need to be vigilant, attentive and careful so that marital life and relationship will be for his glory and for our peaceful existence. Christians must make family life a community of hope, love, assurance, care and renewal so that it will give other hopeless families a message of hope. Scripture holds out great hope for the restoration of marriage by encouraging parents to raise their children in integrity and permanency (Deuteronomy 6:2-9). In the book of 'Song of Songs', King Solomon affirms the beauty of sexual union and love within the marriage in terms of enthusiasm, loyalty and truthfulness. It offers a strategy for marriage in terms of mutual submission, devotion, love and discipline for children that does not alienate them from marriage.

Someone once said, "Keep your eyes wide open before marriage, half shut afterwards." Keep your eyes wide open before marriage means marriage is non-transferable. It is major decision once you took a decision to marry someone, it is a lifelong decision. Therefore one need discernment to understand its divine power. If we want the blessing of a contented, cheerful, happy and permanent marriage, keeping both eyes open before marriage. Half shut afterwards means only focus your life on your spouse even if she is not the one you dreamt about. You have to stick with your spouse and no one else. Never try to major on minor things. One must develop the characters of tolerance, longsuffering, forbearing, forgetting and forgiving for the success and permanence of the marriage relationship.

According to Meghnad Desai, an economist and author writes, "Several successful men marry more than once as if they are trying out different versions of what they want. Celebrity husbands are fawned over by women fans, who look critically at their spouses, hence the pressure on the wife to be a perfect arm candy."[3] Both husband and wife must hold on to their confidence and work on their own prospective, potential and strengths.

Justice Gambhir of the Delhi High Court, stressed the importance of a healthy sexual relationship between normal couples. "The sanctity of sexual relationship and its role in re-invigorating the bond of marriage is getting diluted and as a consequence more and more couples are seeking divorce due to sexual incompatibility and absence of sexual satisfaction." Again, he noted, "That 'the twain shall become one flesh, so that they are no more twain but one'... (is the) real purpose of marriage and sexual intercourse is a means..."[4] He clearly stated his verdict in few apt words - 'sanctity of sexual relationship,' 'sexual incompatibility,' and 'the purpose of marriage.' These are all incongruent with the Christian marriage principles. He highlighted this oneness in his verdict.

The first and foremost criterion for a successful Christian family is 'praying together with your spouse.' Set aside quality time each day for prayer and spend quiet time with your spouse. The time spent together is considered as a spiritual exercise. This time can be used as a time of spiritual and mental intimacy with each other in the presence of God. This intimacy will help the couple grow more mature together in every aspect of their life.

Secondly, 'set aside quality time in reading, meditating and studying the word of God' together. This might be called as a time of devotion or solitude and use it as a good time for personal assessment, evaluation, reflection, refinement, adaption and rectification. The time spent with God can enhance both personal and marital life.

Thirdly, the couple should always 'make the major decisions together with one spirit.' Make it a habit of taking every decision together if possible, especially major and important ones in marital life.

Fourthly, it is important to 'attend church together for regular worship services.' Find a suitable place of worship where you and your spouse will not only attend together, but enjoy areas of mutual interest, growing spiritually together, serve in a ministry and make friends together. Never skip the church service unless you are sick or on account of an emergency. Many young people forego attending church today saying, 'Monday through Saturday we work. Sunday is the only day to do chores and the only occasion when spouses get to spend time together.' This will be impossible for many if one is working away from home or living in different places.

Why do a number of couples face adverse consequences like family disputes, disharmony, broken relationships, separation or divorce? Irregular time factors in the work area is one reason. The problem of childcare when both parents are working is also a common problem. Due to busy schedules, there is very little time to spend together or pray together. Therefore, so many unnecessary elements spring up like lack of trust and respect and love for one another. Misunderstandings misinterpretations and confusion also contribute to deterioration of the marriage bond.

The only thing that God acknowledges to be 'not good' is the unfinished creation of man as a single being. Then God said "is not good that the man should be alone; I will make a helper suitable for him" (Genesis 2:18). After creation, God himself acknowledged that without a female, man is incomplete and imperfect. With man alone or two men (homosexual) or two females (lesbian) there could be no procreation or companionship. Probably companionship is possible in homosexual and lesbian ties, but procreation is not possible. It can be argued that, perhaps, in God's mind, during the time of creation, he put a high value on procreation. Without this, God's intension of marriage is incomplete and imperfect. Therefore, God created a woman for man's companionship, fellowship and procreation. This is for mutual pleasure and enjoyment.

The Bible compares marriage between a man and woman to the relationship between Christ and his Church. Husbands are to love their wives in the same way that Christ loved the church. Christ loved the church sacrificially and without any conditions.

Healthy marriage involves great affection towards the spouse. The man (Adam) said, "This is now bone of my bones and flesh of my flesh; she shall be called woman, for she was taken out of man" (Genesis 2:23). Adam instantly sensed an intimacy towards Eve. He knew that God had created her from his rib and she was not just another of God's creation for him. She was made from his own flesh. He acknowledged that she was solely created for him; therefore he must love her more dearly. Marriage will never stay alive without genuine love towards each other. Therefore love is an essential factor in the marriage contract for smooth and lifelong relationships.

Marriage involves commitment, loyalty and devotion. For this reason a man will leave his father and mother and be united to his wife, and they will become one flesh (Genesis 2:24). God makes a startling statement about marriage that many overlook that they shall become one flesh. He reveals two things which the man must leave his father and mother, and cleave unto his wife. This is extensively discussed in previous chapters. The couple, in holy matrimony, has become one and they are now each other's priority.

Marriage involves accountability. The man and his wife were both naked, and they felt no shame (Genesis 2:25). This verse seems so strange, but it is significant. Before sin entered into their hearts, there was no feeling of shame or any sort of sinful thoughts. They were comfortable in their nakedness. Many marriages have failed due to unfaithfulness and disloyalty. But love towards the spouse, remaining committed to each other, make marriage beautiful and long lasting.

The need of the hour for all churches and members of the church is to ensure that strong teachings are given on Christ-centred marriages; further these families should be well supported continuously to lead exemplary family lives. This can be achieved to a great extent by providing post-marital counselling which will enlighten a fresh look at marriage. It will also help them to clarify misconceptions on marriage and accept healthy teachings which will produce good fruits in the days to come.

As days go, marital discord has alarmingly become common and the number of divorces is on the rise; hence the need of the hour is pre and post-marital counselling. Children at a very young age should be taught about Christ-centred family. This can be achieved through the exemplary lives of parents, Sunday school classes, youth meetings, pulpit sermons, Bible studies, seminars etc. However, before marriage the couple must earnestly prepare and plan to enter into a Christ-designed family. Continued support by the church, post-marital counselling, and sermons from the pulpit are some ways which can sustain them in their marriage if they have deep rooted faith.

Von Gagern, says, "Often it is only through his wife that the husband becomes truly a man; and through her husband that the wife gains true womanhood."[5] How true is it? In a healthy marriage both husband and wife strive for a stable and a transparent relationship. They correct or complement each other which make a lot of difference in sustaining a happy marriage. Then the question comes into our mind, 'How can I enjoy my marriage'? Again, there is no shortcut for a happy martial relationship. The answer is quite simple - if God the Almighty is the head of the family, couples will enjoy a long lasting relationship.

There are many couples who focus more on personal and professional growth, and they believe that one should concentrate on acquiring higher education, a good job, house with all amenities, car, significant bank balance, etc first and then should get married. Once they establish all this, they may not be able to find a suitable match.

It is noteworthy that many young men decide not to take anything in cash or kind from the girl's parents at the time of marriage but ensure that they will take care and provide for their wives.

In short stability of the marriage does not depend upon:

- how much money is spent on the wedding - wedding dress, ornaments, hall, decoration, entertainment, lighting and sound, transportation, feast etc.

- how many political leaders, business magnets, celebrities, bishops, clergyman, pastors or the number of people attended the services and reception.

- Who conducted the marriage service.

- The family, cultural, religious, socio- economic and religious backgrounds of the bride and bridegroom.

All the above are outwardly expression whereas God's expectation about the couple is their commitment to each through inward action.

The wedding service should be a time of dedication, surrender and submission to the Lord Almighty. In togetherness the families, relatives and friends prayerfully commit the bride and bridegroom in God's hands, the same as how the lad handed over the five small loaves of bread and two small fishes to the hands of Jesus (John 6:9,11). God's blessing is the most important aspect as the couple walk confidently hand in hand 'Down the Aisle' to be a blessing for themselves and for the multitude around them.

HOW ABOUT YOU?

ARE YOU 'DOWN THE AISLE'??

WHAT ABOUT YOUR MARRIAGE AND FAMILY LIFE???

Endnotes

[1] "Over 10,000 students take oath not to marry without parents' consent," *The Times of India*, Ahmedabad: Surat News, February 15, 2019, 5.

[2] 'Family Expectations' Word in Life Bible' (Nashville: Thomas Nelson Publishers, 1998), 77.

[3] "Do successful men make lousy husbands? *Times of India* (Bangalore), 6 May 2012, 4.'Times Life' - Times News Network, anuradha.varma@timesgroup.com

[4] Abhinav Garg, "Healthy sex life necessary for a sound marriage," *Sunday Times of India*, Bangalore, 25 March 2012, 12.

[5] Friedrich E. F. Von Gagern, Der Mensch als Bild: Beiträge zur Anthropologie. 2nd ed. (Frankfurt am Main: Verlag Josef Knecht, 1955), 32.

Bibliography

Books

Adams, Jay. E. *Competent To Counsel*. New Jersey: Presbyterian & Reformed Publishing Co, 1975.

_____*The Christian Counselor's Manual*. New Jersey: Presbyterian & Reformed Publishing Co, 1979.

Akin, Daniel L. *The beauty and blessings of the Christian bedroom*, Song of Solomon 4:1-5:1. Englewood, New Jersey: Devora Publishing Company, 2003.

Aland, K. *The Greek New Testament*. London: United Bible Societies, 1965.

Bosman, H. *Adultery, prophetic tradition and the Decalogue, in Brown, W P* (ed), *The Ten Commandments: The reciprocity of faithfulness*, London: Westminster John Knox, 2004.

Brasch, R. *How Did It Begin?* New York: David McKay Co, 1965.

Browning, D. *The world situation of families: Marriage reformation as a cultural work*. Edinburgh: T & T Clark Ltd, 2001.

Browning, D. World *family trends*, in Gill, R (ed), *The Cambridge Companion to Christian Ethics*, 243-260. Cambridge: Cambridge University Press, 2001.

Brueggemann, W. *Theology of the Old Testament, testimony, dispute, advocacy*. Minneapolis, MN: Fortress Press, 1997.

Church of England. *Something to celebrate: Valuing families in church and society*, London: Church House, 1995.

Clark, Stephen. *Man and Woman in Christ*. Ann Arbor: Servant, 1980.

Douma, J. *The Ten Commandments: Manual for the Christian Life*. Phillipsburg, New Jersey: P & R Publishing, 1996.

Foulkes, F. *Ephesians: An introduction and commentary.* London: Tyndale.1968.

Gill, R. *Moral leadership in a postmodern age.* Edinburgh: T & T Clark, 1997.

Fred, Gettings. *The Book of the Hand.* London: Hamlyn Ltd, 1965.

Gottman, John. *Why Marriages Succeed or Fail.* New York: Simon & Schuster Inc, 1994.

Gottman, John M. *The Seven Principles for Making Marriage Work.* New York: Three Rivers Press, 1999.

Hauerwas, S. *A community of character, toward a constructive Christian social ethic.* London: Notre Dame, 1981.

Heimbach, Daniel R. *True Sexual Morality-Recovering Biblical standards for a culture in Crisis.* Secunderabad: Authentic, 2004.

Heyns, J A. *Teologiese etiek, deel 1.* Pretoria: NG Kerkboekhandel, 1982.

Keane, P S. *Sexual morality: A Catholic perspective.* Dublin: Gill & Macmillan, 1980.

James, Remington McCarthy. Rings through the Ages. New York: Harper & brothers, 1945.

Johnson, Greg & Mike Yorkey. *The Second Decade of Love.* Wheaton: Tyndale House Publishers Inc., 1994.

Kostenberger, A J. *God, marriage and family: Rebuilding the Biblical foundation.* Wheaton, Illinois: Crossway, 2004.

Ketterman, Grace H. *Understanding your child's problems.* Grand Rapids, Michigan: Fleming H. Revel, 1992.

Lewis, C.S. *Mere Christianity.* New York: Simon & Schuster, 1980.

Leupold, H.C. *Exposition of Genesis, Volume 1.* Grand Rapids, Michigan: Baker Book House, 1979.

Marshall, F.H. *Catalogue of the Finger Rings.* British Museum, 1968.

Mc McCormick, P T & Connors, R B. *Facing ethical issues, dimensions of character, choices and community.* New York: Paulist, 2002.

Meurer, Dave. *Good Spouse keeping.* England: Life Journey, 2004.

Murata, Sachiko. *Temporary Marriage (Mut'a) in Islamic Law.* Qum: Ansariyan, 1992.

Mursteinb J, & Glaudinv. *The relationship of marital adjustment to personality: a factor analysis of the interpersonal check list. I. Marriage & Family,* 1966.

Omartian, Stormie. *The power of a Praying Husband.* Hyderabad: Authentic, 2010.

Paul Berdanier & James R. McCarthy. *Rings through the Ages,* New York: Harper & Bros, 1945, np.

Palmer R O. *The Christ of the covenants.* Phillipsburg, New Jersey: Presbyterian and Reformed Publishing Co, *2008.*

Rendtorff, R. *The Covenant formula, an exegetical and theological investigation.* Edinburgh: T & T Clark, 1998.

Russell, Bertrand, *Marriage and Morals.* New York: Liveright, 1970.

Schur, W. C. *Piro; a three-dimensional theory of interpersonal behavior.* New York: Holc, Rinehart & Winsron, 1960.

Sharma, R.N. *Introductory Sociology.* Meerut, U.P: Raj bans Prakashan Mandir, 1975.

Stackhouse, M L. Christian social ethics in a global era: Reforming Protestant views, in *Christian social ethics in a global era.* Nashville, TN: Abingdon, 1995.

Stewart, Charles William. *The Minister as marriage Counselor.* New York Nashville: Abingdon Press, 1961.

Stone, Abraham and Hannah. *A Marriage Manual.* New York: Simon and Schuster, Inc.,1952.

Stott, John. *Issues Facing Christians Today - A major appraisal of contemporary social and moral questions* .Bombay: Gospel Literature Services, 1989.

_____ *The Message of 1 Timothy and Titus.* Downers Grove, Illinois: Inter Varsity Press, 1996.

Vander Walt, B J. *Naby God: Christus en kerk op die drumpel van spiritualiteit.* Potchefstroom: Potchefstroomse Universities vir Christelike Hoër Onderwys, 1999.

Varghese, Thomas. Abuse of women in Indian Christian Families-Role of Clergymen, Church and Theological Institutions. Delhi: Indian Society for Promoting Christian Knowledge (ISPCK), 2013.

_____ By Grace to Graze- A Walk through a Pastor's Life. Delhi: Indian Society for Promoting Christian Knowledge (ISPCK), 2015.

Velema, W. H. *Discussie over menchenrechten.* Apeldoorn: Willem de Zwijgerstichting, 1980.

Vorster, J M. *Ethical perspectives on Human Rights.* Potchefstroom: Potchefstroom Theological Publications, 2004.

Venetia Newall. *Man, Myth and Magic,* ed. Richard Marshall, New York: Cavandish Corp, 1970.

Westberg, Granger, *Premarital Counselling.* New York: National Council of Churches of Christ in USA, 1958.

Wynn, John C. *Pastoral Ministry to Families.* Philadelphia: Westminster Press, 1957.

_____*How Christian Parents Face Family Problems.* Philadelphia: Westminster Press, 1955.

Yedida Kalfon Stillman. *Palestinian Costume and Jewellery.* University of New Mexico Press, Albuquerque, 1979.

Periodicals

Abraham Rees, The Cyclopaedia, Vol. XXX, London: Longman, Hurst, Rees, Orme & Brown, 1819, np.

Artsikhovski, A.V *Great Soviet Encyclopaedia*, NewYork: Macmillan, Vol. 19, 1978.

Churchill Babington. "Rings," *A Dictionary of Christian Antiquities* (London, 1908), vol. 2, p.1794.

Daniel T. Bordeau, "The Practice of Wearing Gold," *Review and Herald*, October 5, 1869.

Douma, J *Seksualiteit en huwelijk.* Kampen: Uitgeverij van den Berg, 1993.

Encyclopaedia Britannica, 11th ed., Vol. XXII, Cambridge, England, 1911, Fedler, K D 2006.

Encyclopaedia of Oriental Philosophy & Religion- A continuing Series Volume 12, Christanity. Edited by N.K.Singh * A.P. Mishra, Globial Vision Pub. House, New Delhi. 2007.

Exploring Christian Ethics, Biblical foundations for morality. Westminster: John Knox.

Goodrichd. W, Ryderr. G. & Raush, H. L. Patterns of newlywed marriage. Presented at the Annual Meeting of the American Psychiatric Association, Atlantic City, N. J., 1966.

Palmer, Paul E. "Christian Marriage: Contract or Covenant?" *Theological Studies* vol. 33, no. 4 (December 1972): 639.

Ryderr G. The facrualizing game: a sickness of psychological research. *Psychological Reports.* 1966.

Ryder, G. & Flint, A. A. Vicissitudes of marital disputes: the Object Matching Test. Presented at the American Orrhopsychiauic Association meeting in St. Louis, Missouri, 1966. T*he Encyclopedia Americana,* 1994 ed., s. v. "Ring," (vol. 23, p.531).

The Catholic Encyclopedia, 1908 edition, s. v. "Rings" (vol. 9, p.59).

The Encyclopedia of World Methodism, 1977 edition, s. v. "Dress" (vol. 2, p.718).

Whang, Y C. Cohabitation or conflict: Greek household management and Christian *Haustafeln*, in Hayes, M A et al. *Religion and Sexuality*. Sheffield: Sheffield Academic Press, 1998.

Dictionary

Henry H. Halley, *Bible Handbook*, Grand Rapids, Michigan: Zondervan Publishing house, 24th Ed., 1965.

Isidore of Seville, *De Ecclesiasticis Officiis* 2, 20, cited in *A Dictionary of Christian Antiquity* (note 19), vol. 2, p.1808.

Moynagh, M Family, in Atkinson, D J (ed) et al, *New Dictionary of ChristianEthics and Pastoral Theology*. Leicester: Inter-Varsity Press, 1995.

Vorster, J M. The attitude of Christ as a principle for modern Christian ethicsseen from a classic Reformed perspective. *Studia Historia Ecclesiasticae,* 2004.